John Haylock

*Loose Connections*

A
ARCADIA BOOKS
LONDON

Arcadia Books Ltd
15–16 Nassau Street
London W1W 7AB

www.arcadiabooks.co.uk

First published in the United Kingdom in 2003
Copyright © John Haylock 2003

John Haylock has asserted his moral right to be identified as the author of this work in accordance with the Copyright, Designs and Patents Act, 1988.

All Rights Reserved. No part of this publication may be reproduced in any form or by any means without the written permission of the publishers.

A catalogue record for this book is available from the British Library.

ISBN 1–900850–77–X

Typeset in Iowan Old Style by Northern Phototypesetting Co. Ltd, Bolton
Printed in the United Kingdom by J W Arrowsmith Ltd. Bristol

Arcadia Books distributors are as follows:

in the UK and elsewhere in Europe:
Turnaround Publishers Services
Unit 3, Olympia Trading Estate
Coburg Road
London N22 6TZ

in the USA and Canada:
Independent Publishers Group
814 N. Franklin Street
Chicago, IL 606 10

in Australia:
Tower Books
PO Box 213
Brookvale, NSW 2100

in New Zealand:
Addenda
Box 78224
Grey Lynn
Auckland

in South Africa:
Quartet Sales and Marketing
PO Box 1218
Northcliffe
Johannesburg 2115

Arcadia Books: *Sunday Times* Small Publisher of the Year 2002/03

*For Gary Pulsifer*

**Also by John Haylock**

*Easter Exchange: Memoirs*
*New Babylon: A Portrait of Irak* (with Desmond Stewart)

Novels

*See You Again*
*It's All Your Fault*
*One Hot Summer in Kyoto*
*A Touch of the Orient*
*Uneasy Relations*
*Doubtful Partners*
*Body of Contention*

Publications in Japan

*Tokyo Sketchbook*
*Choice and Other Stories*
*Japanese Excursions*
*Japanese Memories*
*Romance Trip and Other Stories*

Translations from the French

*Robert de Montesquiou* by Phillippe Jullian (with Francis King)
*Flight into Egypt* by Phillippe Jullian

# Loose Connections

The characters in this light-hearted novel, which has a dark side to it, are an ill-assorted bunch; the story is set mostly in Egypt shortly before the Six Day War with Israel in 1967. Violet, a lesbian millionairess, in order to keep up pretences marries a gay aspirant author, Oliver Brent. Saman, a rich Thai student, falls in love with Joan Webber, his teacher at a Hove language school. Joan is also loved by Violet. To escape the increasingly possessive attentions of Saman and Violet, Joan gets a job at a school near Cairo. Her only English colleague is Ronald Wood, a middle-aged homosexual, who has an Egyptian lover called Khalid. Violet's wealth allows her to act on whims and she is used to having her way. Oliver approves of his wife's sudden desire to winter in Egypt as he has a lover in Cairo. The characters often meet for luncheon at Groppi's Restaurant where the mediocre fare is mitigated by their scintillating and sometimes scurrilous table talk.

Saman arrives in Cairo and Violet's plans to go alone with Joan to Luxor are thwarted. To his dismay, Ronald discovers that he is sharing his lover with Oliver. The tense situation between the Arabs and Israel smoulders in the background until it explodes and upsets the arrangements of the self-centred foreigners, who remain oblivious until they are affected by it. One of the regular lunchers at Groppi's is Cedric, an Egyptophile journalist on a local English newspaper; it is he who brings home to the visitors the seriousness of the situation.

Saman returns to England to continue his studies. When hostilities are on the verge of eruption Violet, Joan, Oliver and Ronald flee in their cars to Libya, where they are confronted with more than they bargained for.

☪

'What news?' asked Cedric Palmer as he joined Ronald Wood at a table in Groppi's Restaurant in the heart of the European quarter of Cairo.

'You're the one who should have news since you work on a newspaper,' replied Ronald. 'I do as a matter of fact have some news. I had a letter yesterday from Oliver Brent.'

'Never heard of him,' muttered Cedric, who was perusing the menu. He looked up at his friend. 'Oh yes I have. Of course I have. I met him when he was writing his book about Cairo. That must have been three or four years ago.'

'You mean *Among the Minarets?*'

'I never read it,' admitted Cedric. 'I believe it was a success.'

'Very much so. A bestseller.'

'D'you know Oliver Brent well?'

'I knew him at school and we've kept in touch, but not much more than an occasional letter and the exchange of Christmas cards with messages attached. I've been abroad most of the time.'

'I can't think why he didn't write to me,' said Cedric, who seemed indignant and hurt. 'I helped him a lot with his book. Didn't he marry an heiress?'

'Yes. Violet Darnton. She inherited a fortune when her father died.'

'She didn't accompany him when he was writing that book,' said Cedric, emphasizing the last two words with contempt.

'They often go their own ways,' explained Ronald.

Ronald was slowly consuming the table d'hôte luncheon and was sitting at a banquette table with his back to the wall. The two friends met regularly and whoever arrived first took the banquette seat, to the irritation of the other. Both preferred to face the room and watch the suffragis and the other clientele, especially what was called the 'pashas's table' occupied by five or six members of the Faroukian regime, one of whom was said to have been a Minister. Ronald found the suffragis in their flowing jellabas and tarbooshes more interesting than the pashas.

Ronald was approaching fifty, Cedric was ten years older; the former was greying, the latter was balding. Ronald had held unlucrative teaching posts in the Near and Far East, and Cedric was in what might be termed minor journalism. Neither was ambitious. Ronald was 'performing', as he put it, at Nile College in Maadi, a southern suburb of Cairo, once a haven for the rich; now the estates of the landowners had been expropriated and the formerly wealthy were compelled to watch carefully their depleted hoard of piastres. It was 1966. Nasser was at the height of his powers: popular and respected. By the young he was loved because he had given them hope and made them proud to be Egyptian. In 1956 the Suez campaign had been a disaster all round: for the French, the British and the Egyptians; but the last had been told it was a victory for them since the old colonial powers had been forced to withdraw.

'Is it a meatless day?' asked Cedric.

'No.'

'What are you having?'

'The beef.'

'Don't fancy beef; it's probably water buffalo. I'll have an omelette.'

'It's not on the menu,' warned Ronald.

'Surely the cook can make an omelette even if it isn't on the menu. Have you met Oliver Brent's wife?'

'I met her at her wedding at Tring where she had a huge house, a nineteenth century pile. I happened to be in England and Oliver invited me. It was an informal affair. No top hats, frock coats, or white wedding dresses. I hardly spoke to Violet, the bride. She's a big woman, pleasant looking, no beauty. She seemed shy.'

'Shy people,' pronounced Cedric, who tended to be sententious, 'are often aggressive.' He turned to the waiter, who was hovering by the table. 'A demi-carafe of red wine, please, and a tomato omelette, and please see that the tomatoes are peeled.'

The suffragis fetched and carried dishes from the kitchen to the dining-room; the waiters, who were of European origin, took the orders; they wore white jackets and made-up bow-ties.

Violet Darnton's father, Clarence, had wide business interests: oil, shipping, steel, banking and insurance. His two bitter disappointments were: he had no son, and his wife had died giving birth to Violet. After losing his wife, of whom he was inordinately fond, making money became an obsession. He concentrated all his efforts on increasing his fortune, which was large enough anyway; he didn't know what else to do. Clarence was born in 1861, the son of Vincent Darnton, a land-owner and squire whose gambling on his own horses at point-to-points in Cambridgeshire and flat racing at Newmarket forced him to mortgage his property and let his house, a charming Georgian mansion rebuilt in 1828 by his father.

Vincent married Mabel Longfield, the daughter of a City timber merchant. Soon after the birth of a son, Clarence, he died of tuberculosis. Clarence was brought up by his mother and her family. The estate in Cambridgeshire was sold (Mabel hated the country, country pursuits and country society) for less than it was worth. There was a slump in agriculture, and Mabel's family considered it best to get rid of the mortgage and the estate: ready money could make more money, a mortgaged property was a burden. Clarence was taught the ways and the guiles of a City merchant. He soon evinced the aptitude which his maternal grandfather had possessed, and after leaving Harrow he joined the family firm. He did well, beyond the expectations of his grandfather. Soon Clarence realized that the firm had become hidebound and he urged his now elderly grandparent to expand. With reluctance he agreed and by 1914 Clarence had created one of the most prosperous companies in the City, with interests far beyond the dreams of the old timber merchant. Clarence did not marry until 1910 when he was forty-nine. He was too busy.

His wife, Margaret, who was thirty-two when he married her, had been entrapped by her widowed mother, who took a long time to die. Clarence met Margaret Bannerham on the train from Victoria to Reigate, where they both lived. It was unusual for Clarence to speak to a stranger but there was something about Margaret that attracted him: her demureness, perhaps, her inexperience, the sheltered life she had been forced to lead. When they struck up a conversation on the train, Clarence learnt that she had paid one of her rare visits to London to see her solicitor in Bedford Row about her mother's will and about the three-storey Victorian house she had inherited.

'If you'd like my advice, I'll give it to you.'

Margaret shyly accepted the offer.

In six weeks they were married. Their respective houses in Reigate were put on the market and Clarence bought a large house with extensive grounds at Tring. Margaret had never imagined herself as a chatelaine but she was intelligent and quickly learned to live up to the challenge of running a considerable property.

The satisfaction of proving that she was capable of dealing with the demands that fell on her shoulders ended after six years of marriage (neither she nor her husband cared for the sexual act: she found it distasteful, he a tedious operation that interrupted his thoughts about business). She became pregnant but died in 1916 giving birth to a daughter. Clarence was distraught, more so than if Margaret had produced a son. The child was christened Margaret Violet but called Violet as Clarence couldn't bear to hear his wife's name uttered by nurses, governesses and relations. He worked even harder in the City (his age and his work precluded him from being called up when conscription was introduced in 1916) and continued to manage his businesses astutely. He did not suffer any great losses in the slump after the war, and when he died in 1938 he left a considerable fortune.

Violet was educated at a private girls' school. She inherited her paternal grandfather's love of horses. She begged her indulgent father to buy her a mount, which he did, and she became a capable horsewoman.

She was about to go up to Cambridge when her father had a fatal heart attack. An unemotional woman blessed with self-control, she was dry-eyed at the funeral, which took place at Tring. Although Violet was up to dealing with the problems her father's demise had caused and, having spent much of her youth alone with servants, faced the prospect of living alone with equanimity, she agreed to the suggestion of her mother's cousin, Evelyn Cartwright, that she move into the house at Tring with her bosom friend, Martha Hopkins. There was plenty of room and Evelyn had been kind to Violet when a girl, inviting her to various entertainments in London. Clarence had always been too occupied to provide amusements for his daughter.

Both Evelyn and Martha were in their sixties. They had been sharing a flat in Lexham Gardens in Kensington. Martha had just retired from her job as a social worker. Evelyn's small private income had enabled her to do unpaid work in the parish. She had, though, fallen out with the new young vicar, who did not conduct the services in the way she thought was correct. Both Evelyn and Martha were ready to move. Clarence's death had been timely in that it provided the two friends with an opportunity to do so.

Violet's head ruled her heart. At the same time she was compassionate and could be kind; she was aware of the debt of gratitude she owed Evelyn. During her father's lifetime she had occasionally persuaded him to allow her to invite Evelyn and Martha to stay at Tring, reminding him of Evelyn's goodness to her. Clarence had reluctantly agreed to these visitations, recognizing the fact that Evelyn had been generous to his daughter. He did not, though, behave gallantly towards the two devoted friends. When they were in the house he either stayed at his London club or returned to Tring for dinner, after which he would retire to his study. Clarence was possessive of his daughter and did not like her to have friends. He called Evelyn and Martha 'those two lesbian horrors'. Violet had defended them. In fact, neither of the two friends knew anything about lesbianism. Their relationship was platonic.

When, during the school holidays, Violet had stayed with Evelyn and Martha in London, she had not been aware of the managerial side of Evelyn's character. It seemed natural to Violet as a child and a guest that Evelyn should run things, and when the two friends stayed at Tring Evelyn did not reveal her domineering trait because, Violet realized later, her mother's cousin was afraid of Clarence.

Soon after Evelyn and Martha moved into the house at Tring, Evelyn started to give orders to the servants and make suggestions about the management of the estate. Violet was not a weak character and she would countermand any interference. This resulted in periodical clashes with Evelyn, who, crushed, would go to her bedroom in tears, tears which did not move Violet at all.

Violet was relieved when the academic year began and she could escape to Cambridge.

Being no beauty – her height was against her and her flat chest did not help, nor did her wispy brown hair, but she had a generous smile and a benevolent air – Violet realized that her main attraction was her wealth, and she was therefore wary of approaches by fellow undergraduates. At the same time she knew that she was what her father had found repugnant: a lesbian horror. She discovered during her first year that the company she felt most at ease with was that of men who were queer. She got on better with them than with normal females. She met Oliver Brent after a lecture – they were both reading history – and struck up a friendship with him. She liked him for two reasons: he didn't seem to be interested in her money and he appeared to be complaisant. He found her good company after her wall of shyness had been broken down. They laughed at the same things. Of course, the fact that Violet was rich did not put Oliver off and he, a passive character, liked to be led.

☪

'Tell me,' said Cedric across the table to Ronald, 'about Oliver Brent's wife. He never mentioned her to me.'

'She was the daughter of Clarence Darnton, the millionaire industrialist, who died just before the war.'

'How old would she be now?'

'Let me see.' Ronald put a crooked finger to his lips. 'It's 1966, so she must be 46 if she was 18 when she went up to Cambridge.'

'He'd be roughly the same age,' said Cedric. 'Pushing 50. He was pleasant enough when he was here writing his book. Overweight. He ate a lot and drank quite a bit. Queer. Perhaps that's why he never mentioned that he was married.'

'Probably. Married queers often don't admit they've got a wife to birds of the same feather. But she's queer, I gather. At the wedding the guests were a very mixed lot.'

'How d'you mean?'

'There were one or two queers I knew and some rather masculine women. One old trout wore a bow tie.'

'Why did they marry?'

'It was a *mariage de convenance*,' explained Ronald. 'He wanted to be respectable, to be able to say he was married when asked, and she wanted to ward off pesterers after her money.'

'Wasn't Oliver after her money?'

'I suppose he was. Writing doesn't bring in all that much, even if you've written a best seller like *Among the Minarets*. It put him on the map, but his novel *Blatant Folly* was a flop and took him off the map. As you probably know, Cedric, Oliver has an Egyptian lover and—'

'I didn't know. He never confided in me.'

'He met him in Ezbekieh Gardens and he is the main reason for his revisiting Cairo. And his wife is in love with Joan Webber, who teaches at Nile College. I only know her slightly; she hasn't been here long. Apparently – I learnt all this from Oliver's letter about his and his wife's trip. I surmise that Joan came here to escape from Violet's clutches.'

'Who's Violet?'

'Oliver's wife.'

'So the wealthy couple are coming here for sex.'

'Yes, but they pretend that they're coming to study some aspect or other of Egypt.'

'Is Joan Webber happy at Nile College?'

'As I said, I hardly know her. I think that one of the teachers, Adnan, has the hots for her. He's asked me about her. He's very good looking. I wouldn't mind—'

'But you have Khalid.'

'Yes, but . . .'
'Where are the fabled couple going to stay?'
'At the Semiramis.'
'I'd like to see them; after all I did meet Oliver.'

☪

Oliver Brent was the son of a doctor of medicine, who had a practice in Bournemouth. He and his wife moved to the seaside resort soon after their marriage in 1914 from Blackheath, which neither of them had liked. Oliver was born in 1919. His father's practice prospered. Oliver grew up in a large Edwardian house among the pines, not far from the pier. He was educated at a local preparatory school, a minor public school in Dorset and at Cambridge University.

At his prep school he was a weekly boarder, going home at weekends. One evening he discovered Lucas, an older boy, lying in the bath and playing with his erect cock. Oliver was fascinated. At first he thought that there was something wrong with Lucas, but soon he realized that it was natural and that his cock could become big too. In the dormitory the boys played a game called 'Birth Rate'. The head of the dorm would announce, 'Birth rate going up'. Whereupon the boys, not knowing quite why, would jump on top of one another and bounce up and down. On the command 'Birth rate going down', the boys would regain their own beds.

There was a copse at the bottom of Dr Brent's garden and Oliver and Ken Smith would play there. Mrs Brent was not on social terms with the Smiths. Mr Smith was 'in trade', owning a successful furniture store, but Mrs Brent allowed Oliver and Ken to be playmates as her son was lonely. Ken, who had two older brothers, was more au fait with wordly matters than Oliver. When Ken told Oliver about sex in more detail than he had learnt at school, Oliver at once said, 'Let's try it.'

'It's dangerous,' admonished Ken.

'Never mind. Let's do it.'

Ken wouldn't consent to Oliver's suggestion. He did, though, allow Oliver to play with his cock, but he wouldn't touch Oliver's.

In the first class at his public school Oliver sat next a boy with a sallow complexion who put his hand inside Oliver's trouser pocket and tossed him off. Oliver always remembered the wet feeling in his crotch when in the middle of the morning the junior school did PT. He feared that dampness would show through his trousers; it didn't. This incident (it was the first time anyone had felt his prick) lingered in the back of his mind all his life; now and then it would come forward into his consciousness. Sex continued to play a part, perhaps too important a part, during his schooldays. He would have 'pashes' on other boys, some of whom would reciprocate; others remained a dream.

Oliver went up to Cambridge in the autumn of 1938, having left school without regret and without distinction in the December of the previous year. He spent eight months in Tours learning French, which he had only half-learned at school. It was his mother's wish that he should spend a spell abroad – 'So you don't go up to the university as a green schoolboy,' she had said. At the Institut Francais in Tours Oliver met a group of American girls. They intrigued him. They were so different from their English counterparts: better dressed, friendlier, franker, almost brash. One in particular attracted him, a dark girl with large black eyes, and with her he had a boyish affair, which was never consummated. She was willing but Oliver couldn't go through with it. He was beginning to realize that women didn't attract him physically and that his schoolboy romances represented his true nature.

At Cambridge in the autumn of 1938 war was in the air. It was an unsettling period. Chamberlain's 'Peace in Our Time' was mocked in a November 5th parade by three undergraduates dressed as old men about to expire holding up a banner bearing the Prime Minister's fatal words. When war was declared the following September Oliver stayed up to finish Part I of his Tripos.

It was during this uncertain period that Oliver met Violet Darnton after a lecture in Trinity College. He was attracted by her attitude, her way of thinking; and her lack of feminine appeal didn't bother him. He hadn't realized that she was a woman of wealth. She didn't behave as if she could buy the Ritz or hire a private train. She was shy, as was he. Both of them disliked parties. Oliver had found a woman with whom he could have a platonic relationship. The fact that sex played no part in that relationship was a strength. There were no jealousies. Neither of them had affairs, although now and then Oliver took himself off to London where he paid for the services of a male whore. He did not mention these escapades to Violet, who never wanted to talk about sex.

In the summer of 1940, Oliver was called up and eventually commissioned in an infantry regiment. Violet volunteered for the auxiliary London Fire Brigade. Their paths separated. They met again in Cairo in 1943. Oliver had a job in the Allied Liaison Office of the headquarters of the British Forces in the Middle East, and Violet, through a friend of her father's in the Foreign Office, had joined the British Council in Egypt. The two had kept up a correspondence so their both being in Cairo was no surprise to either of them.

☪

The marriage between Violet and Oliver took place in England after the war when they were both civilians again. Oliver had not been able to decide what to do. His father had retired after suffering a stroke and his mother devoted all her time to her husband and running the house now bereft of servants except for a daily. Life in Bournemouth was unbearably boring. Violet solved Oliver's problem by suggesting that they get married, which they did, quietly, in Tring. By now they knew each other's sexual tastes, but they rarely referred to them.

'I suppose you can call marrying money having an occupation,' Oliver's father had said. Neither parent attended the wedding. His father was too frail; his mother wouldn't leave her husband, not even for such an important occasion.

The house at Tring had been requisitioned by the army during the war. The two horses had to be found new homes, and Violet's cousin and her bosom pal Martha had been moved into a cottage on the estate. After the military had given up the property, Violet busied herself with the task of supervising its refurbishment, and when this was complete she married Oliver.

Soon after the wedding Oliver, with Violet's help, revisited Cairo and wrote his book about the minarets of the great city. Half of Violet's fortune was in America (placed there by her prudent father) so she was not affected by the British currency control. Interwoven with the history of the buildings and their architecture were colourful vignettes of life in Cairo, and it was these that sold the book. The sales, though, didn't amount to a large sum, made him decide to be a writer, and with Violet's financial backing he was able to take up writing and not think of another career. He also thought that having a wife would help. His second book, *Blatant Folly*, was a novel set in the Egyptian capital and based on his private experiences when writing his first book. His sexual experiences had been homosexual; in his story he changed some of the men into women and vice versa. It was not possible to change his Egyptian friend, Khalid, into a woman so he changed himself into one. The 'blatant folly' was an English girl's passion for a dashing Egyptian army officer.

Violet's object in marrying was self-protection and respectability, but after she had come across Joan Webber, a teacher, whom she ran into in London at the Old Vic, she became less cautious about her tastes. She showered Joan with presents, invitations to Tring, trips to Paris. Joan, dazzled by Violet's apparent wealth, but puzzled by Oliver's presence at Tring submitted not very enthusiastically to the older woman's cajolements.

'Won't he mind?' Joan once asked Violet when they were in bed together in the Tring house.

'*C'est un mariage blanc,*' explained Violet.

Oliver and Violet had separate apartments in the mansion at Tring. There were days when they entertained privately and although in the same house never met; on others they would meet on neutral ground, as they called the downstairs rooms, which consisted of two drawing-rooms, a library and a dining-room. Violet ran the house and the grounds. Oliver sat either in his quarters or in the library tussling with his third book. When the couple were alone they would occupy the ground floor, sitting in one of the drawing-rooms and eating in the dining-room. Violet sometimes did the cooking but more often it was done by one of the two women who helped in the house. Sometimes they would jointly entertain neighbours. Violet bought new horses and carried on with her riding. Oliver wouldn't go near a horse.

Oliver's thoughts were often taken up with memories of his Egyptian friend. He would spend much of the morning day-dreaming about Khalid. He would pinch his left nipple hard and masturbate. On some mornings he would write not much more than a sentence.

The meetings between Oliver and Violet on neutral territory were cordial and warm. They were fond of each other in their way. They would laugh at themselves and their odd existence together.

Violet mitigated her plain looks with a benign expression. She wore no make-up on her slightly ruddy face and kept her hair cropped short. Her clothes were conservative but well cut; they came from an expensive London couturier. She was shy but she had presence and there was confidence in her movements and her speech. She was taller than Oliver but not wider. Oliver was squat. He allowed his dark locks to grow so he had a full head of hair, but they did not straggle down to his shoulders. He too dressed well. He went to his father's tailor in Madox Street, which his parent had long given up. Together Violet and Oliver looked a well-turned-out couple. They didn't exude wealth but they gave the impression of having no monetary worries.

They mentioned to each other their private affairs but did not elaborate on them. Oliver knew about Violet's craze for

Joan Webber and Violet was aware of her husband's affection for Khalid and his temporary liaisons with young Englishmen, who were sometimes invited to Tring.

☪

Joan Webber, fair-haired, blue-eyed, had a round, cheerful face and a smile that turned up the corners of her mouth. Her friends would call her buxom, her acquaintances, well-covered; she didn't have any enemies as far as she knew, but had she, they might have called her fat – plump would have been fairer.

Her father ran a chemist's shop in Norbury. Joan, an intelligent girl, won a scholarship to London University and on graduation got a teaching post at a language school in Hove. A Chinese-Thai, who came from a rich Bangkok family, paid court to Joan. At first she resisted his persistent invitations to dinner, to the cinema, to the theatre, to London, to go for drives in his Triumph Sports. He would wait for her until her classes were over and, when she appeared, offer her a lift to her flat. At last she gave in to his pleadings. She was attracted by him. He was so neat in his movements. She liked his sleek black hair, his dark eyes which almost disappeared when he gave his generous smile. She often thought of him when she was alone in bed and wondered what he would be like and how he would do it. She was not a virgin. She had had two experiences at university, both times when she was drunk after a party; her partners on those occasions had been callow and clumsy. She was sure that Saman, as he was called, would treat her gently and not like the others who, perhaps because of guilt, had hurried away after they'd come. Saman's skin was a pale honey colour, his wrists and arms were glabrous and she liked that, no tuft of hair peeped out of his open-necked shirt. She had found distasteful the hairy bodies of the two Englishmen she had allowed to seduce her. Saman's straight little nose suited his round face and did not dominate his other features like many a Western beak.

One morning in class Joan mentioned that there was an excellent production of 'A Midsummer Night's Dream' at the Old Vic in London and that she longed to see it. A few days later Saman presented her with a ticket for the play on the evening of the following Saturday.

'I can't go,' she said.

'Why not?' Saman asked. 'Saturday. No work.'

'How can I get back?'

'I have two ticket. We go together. I drive.'

Joan was hesitant. Teachers were not encouraged to accept favours from students, but this chance to see the play was too tempting to miss.

In the theatre she sat next to a large, plain, well-dressed woman of matronly age on whose other side was a portly man, whose head was covered by a mop of dark hair streaked with strands of grey; his face bore a kindly expression; his mouth was weak, his voice precious. The woman kept glancing at Joan and when their eyes met Joan received an enigmatic smile and a slight nod. Puzzled and embarrassed, Joan studied her programme; Saman, unaware, gazed at the darkened stage and jogged his left knee.

In the interval, the older woman invited Joan and Saman for a drink.

At the end of the play (Saman had slept through most of it) Oliver asked Joan and Saman to dine with them at Le Caprice. Joan hesitated, saying, 'We've got to get back to Brighton.' She never liked saying Hove.

'No work tomorrow,' Saman reminded her. 'It not matter what time we get back to Hove. Late better. No traffic.'

In the Ladies at Le Caprice, Violet, spurred on by the *coup de foudre* Joan had given her, overcame her inherent shyness and gave the young teacher her visiting card. 'Do ring. We'd love you to come and stay at Tring,' she said. Joan, not having a card, gave Violet her telephone number. When they got back to their table Oliver was talking animatedly to Saman. Violet was not surprised that her husband was clearly taken with the young Thai.

That night Joan succumbed to Saman's beguiling manner and allowed him to spend the night with her in her basement flat in Hove. He proved to be all that she had imagined he would be: gentle, considerate and exciting. During the next few weeks she realized that she was falling in love with the Chinese-Thai from Bangkok. Saman began to spend more nights in Joan's flat than he did in his own apartment.

An advertisement in the *Times Educational Supplement* for a post at a school in Maadi near Cairo attracted Joan's attention. Escape might be wise. She applied for the job and, after an interview at the Egyptian Embassy in London, was accepted. She resigned from the language school to the dismay of Saman. Being two years older and having been his teacher, Joan did not find it difficult to tell him of her plans; also, because of her lower middle-class upbringing she felt superior to him, a Chinese. She knew this was wrong but it was in her nature to feel so.

'Why you go?' he demanded crossly.

'I want a change.'

'Change from me?'

'No, not that.'

'I very sad.'

'It's sweet of you to be sad, Saman, but—'

'I come Cairo to see you,' he said fiercely.

Joan wanted to say, 'Please don't', but she said, 'That would be lovely.'

'You mean it?'

Joan substituted the 'No' she wished to emit for, 'Of course, darling.'

'I love you, Joan.'

'I love you too.'

'Why you go then?'

'I want to think over our love. I feel it would be good for us to be apart for a while.'

'I no understand. If you love me, you must stay. You must go with me to Bangkok.'

'I'd love to and perhaps I will, but I need to think about it before I decide. It's a difficult decision to make.'

'Difficult to love me?'

'No, no, not that. But—'

'Egypt dangerous place. Not good to go there.'

Joan found she had to steel herself to tell Violet her plans. It was like admitting some transgression to a parent. Unlike Saman, Violet could be formidable. She feared her wrath. During a weekend in Tring (she told Saman she was going to Norbury to see her parents) Joan informed Violet that she was going to Egypt. To her surprise Violet said, 'How splendid! Oliver and I are going there for the winter, when there is not much to do on the estate, and anyway the manager, Mr Jenkins, will be here and he is capable. I love Cairo. I was there in the war. So was Oliver. We'll meet then. How gorgeous! I was wondering how I was going to break the news to you. We're not going till November. The Egyptians are sweet.'

Joan wished she had applied for a job in Japan that was also advertised in the *Times Educational Supplement*; it was too late to do so now.

☾⋆

In mid-November Oliver and Violet motored to Marseilles in their new Jaguar and embarked on the Karadeniz, a Turkish ship that was scheduled to call at Genoa, Naples, Piraeus and Beirut on her voyage to Alexandria. In Naples, while Violet and Oliver were having an after-lunch coffee in the Galleria, Oliver found himself eyeing a young man who was standing in the doorway of a haberdasher's opposite the café. Violet noticed the concupiscent glances exchanged between her husband and the young man. She rose. 'I'm going back to the ship,' she said. 'We sail at nine. For God's sake be careful.'

Oliver wasn't careful. However, the young haberdasher turned out to be all that one could have desired. He took Oliver to a nearby apartment, behaved perfectly and accepted Oliver's tip graciously. There was a spring in Oliver's step as he mounted the gangway of the Karadeniz. He was just in time for dinner. Violet was already at the table. 'Thank God you're back!' she said. 'I had visions of you lying in the gutter with your throat cut, or in gaol, or robbed of your money, watch, ring, passport and everything, and unable to get back to the ship.'

Oliver laughed. 'Nothing like that. He was a very decent fellow.'

'You were lucky.'

'I was.'

'I do think it's rash to make random pick-ups like that.'

'What about Joan?' asked Oliver. 'Wasn't she—'

'You're not comparing Joan with a Neapolitan counter-jumper, are you?'

'She was a pick-up.'

'A respectable one.'

'Mine was respectable.'

'How you can go off with someone you don't know is beyond my comprehension. How can you be so recklessly reprehensible?'

'Don't be such a hypocrite, Violet. You followed Joan into the loo at Le Caprice.'

'Yes. All we did was exchange addresses.'

'You could have done that at the table.'

'In front of her boyfriend? How absurd you are!'

'You were a long time in there.'

'She didn't have a card. I had to write down her telephone number.'

The waiter appeared to replenish their wine glasses, and the repartee ended. Oliver knew that his wife's criticism was a tease prompted by envy.

In Beirut, Violet, part of whose fortune was in American stocks, collected funds for their Egyptian sojourn from the local American Express. Taking advantage of her father's shrewd pecuniary sense, she had had the money sent directly from New York. Violet had no compunction about evading the restrictions imposed by the Treasury. 'It's my money,' she said. 'I shall use it as I like.' Oliver, who benefited from his father-in-law's financial acumen, thoroughly approved.

They remembered their journey to Marseilles more for the meals they ate than the places they stayed in: the langoustines at Evreux, the *poitrine de veau farcie* at Brive, the traditional table d'hôte at Cordes consisting of hot lentil pâté and wild boar.

There were only two other passengers in first class on the Karadeniz. One of them was a Turkish woman, who smoked continuously and talked incessantly to the barman; the other was a Spanish woman of about 30. She sat alone in the lounge without anything to read.

'Why don't you speak to her?' Violet asked her husband. 'She looks lonely.'

'She's more your cup than mine, dear.'

Oliver rose and made a tour of the ship. In second class were a few bourgeois couples with their children. The mothers were busy trying to control their offspring, the fathers sat about twiddling their rosaries. The third class was alive with Spanish and Arab students. The Spaniards played cards noisily; the Arabs were absorbed in songs by Oom Kalthoom played on a tape. The great Egyptian singer's lamentations were listened to with reverence. During his tour Oliver received no glad eyes from anyone.

'This is the dullest of voyages,' he said to Violet on his return to the first-class lounge.

'I don't know what you expected,' replied Violet. 'A shipboard romance?'

'No, dear. Third class seems livelier than the other classes.'

'Perhaps we should have gone third.'

'I don't think you would have liked sharing a cabin or queueing for meals.'

Oliver knew Beirut, having visited the city several times during his stay in Cairo. After dinner at the Lucullus Restaurant, he suggested to Violet that she go back to the ship.

'Where are you going then?' she asked suspiciously. 'Not in search of adventure, I hope.'

'I want to look up someone I know. A woman actually. She works in a bar.'

'I'll come with you.'

'It's not your sort of place.'

'I don't care what sort of place it is,' said Violet, firmly. 'I'm coming with you.'

Reluctantly Oliver concurred.

They took a taxi to the Chateaubriand Bar in the Bourj, the main square in the old part of the city. Behind the bar stood a middle-aged French woman. Hair dyed blonde, voluble, energetic, a cigarette between her lips, she looked younger than her 55 years. She was what homosexuals call a 'queens' moll', a cosy character whom the younger clientele called 'Maman'. On seeing Oliver enter the bar she cried out, 'Oli, *mon cher, mon amour!*' Violet, who lagged behind, gave a faint, diffident smile.

'Marianne, this is my wife,' announced Oliver.

'Enchantée, madame.'

The French woman showed no surprise.

Oliver and Violet sat at the bar. Instead of giving Oliver the latest gossip, which he was dying to hear, about the antics of various acquaintances, Marianne talked of Monsieur Joseph, the owner of the bar, and his Czech wife, whom he had recently married. *'Elle ne parle pas le francais, pas un mot,'* she said. She went on to relate that Monsieur Joseph had gone to Prague and met his future wife – *'c'était tout arrangé, j'en suis sure'* – and married her – *'Monsieur Joseph est bête.'* Marianne surmized that the Czech lady thought she had married a rich Arab, a sheikh, not the proprietor of a bar in a sleazy quarter of the Lebanese capital. Tactlessly, Marianne opined that it was a mistake for *'les gens comme ça'* to marry, then glancing at Violet she quickly added, *'Ca dépend naturellement. Pour Monsieur Joseph c'était une grande erreur.'* She lit another cigarette with the butt of her previous one and repeated, *'Ca dépend. Monsieur avait tort de se marier, mais pour les autres c'est different.'*

The bar was empty. Oliver was relieved that none of his previous Beirut connections was there. If Violet had not insisted on accompanying him it would have been different. Just as they were leaving, however, an old acquaintance of Oliver's appeared on the scene, a young man called Fouad. He greeted Oliver shyly, saying, 'Hello, Mister Oli', and looking at Violet. Oliver said, 'This is my wife, Fouad.' Keeping up his smile of welcome, Fouad shook hands politely with Violet. Like many Muslims Fouad was by no means exclusively homosexual.

It was natural to marry and produce a family. Sex outside marriage was like a pastime, and if one had a foreign friend it could be profitable.

'I'm sorry, Fouad. We've got to go. We're sailing tonight to Egypt.'

'OK, Mister Oli. You come back Beirut?'

'I hope so.' Oliver regretted having to leave Fouad. He had been such a satisfactory lover.

In the taxi back to the docks, Violet asked, 'A close friend?'

'Fairly,' replied Oliver. 'I hope you didn't mind meeting him.'

'Why should I mind? I didn't much care for that old French barmaid. She struck me as a sad person behind her mask of bonhomie.'

'I don't think she's sad,' Oliver said. 'She enjoys life, I think.'

'All those hours standing behind the bar! How can she enjoy life? She seemed the sort of woman who dislikes her own sex. She was so bitchy about the Czech wife of Monsieur Joseph. Does Marianne introduce people?'

'Not actually introduce them. She knows the clientele and will tell one about the reliability of any of them. People confide in her and she enjoys their confidences. She's quite respectable, really. When she had to renew her visa she was treated as a bar hostess by the immigration authorities. She felt humiliated.'

'I suppose it's difficult for the authorities to differentiate between barmaid and bar hostess,' remarked Violet.

As soon as the taxi dropped them at the ship's gangway, Violet and Oliver retired to their cabins. Oliver thought of Fouad and again wished that Violet had not been with him. What a nuisance it was being married!

☪

The ship sailed at midnight and, once out in the open sea, it began to dip and roll. Violet, a bad sailor, moaned; Oliver, a good sailor, slept. The rough weather continued until the calm waters of Alexandria were reached. Violet stayed in her bunk. Oliver struggled about the unsteady bark. He was the only passenger at lunch in the first-class dining-room.

The Karadeniz entered the harbour and anchored a hundred yards from the shore. Violet appeared, white-faced and tired looking. 'Why aren't we docking?' she asked her husband, who was on deck gazing hopefully at the city.

'We're waiting for the immigration officers to come on board.'

'To examine us?'

'Passport control.'

'On board?'

'Convenient for them and for us. If our visas aren't acceptable they won't let us land and we'll have to sail back.'

'Are you serious?'

'Not really.'

Violet was impatient at having to queue with all classes in the first-class lounge for the passport examination. 'This is a bit much,' she complained to Oliver, who, so pleased to have arrived in Egypt, would not brook any hint of criticism.

After a long wait Violet and Oliver sat facing a burly Egyptian immigration officer in battle-dress with a khaki beret sitting squarely on his head. He had a round face, rolling dark eyes and a huge smile. He regarded Oliver. 'You are writer? Name two of your books, please.'

Violet sniggered.

Oliver was grateful for being asked to name only two books as he had only written that number. '*Among the Minarets* and *Blatant Folly*,' he said diffidently.

'Among minaret? What mean among minaret? About birds flying round minaret? About acrobat swinging?' He waved his arms.

The officer and Violet laughed. Oliver gave a weak smile. 'It was,' he protested, 'a serious book about . . .'

The officer was not listening. He turned to Violet, 'How many children you have?'

'None.'

'I am sorry. I have nine. Maybe better not have any.' He sighed and gave his kindly, expansive smile and stamped their passports.

'I liked him,' said Violet as she and Oliver were making their way to their cabins to collect their hand luggage.

'The ordinary Egyptians are charming, full of fun too. I suppose he came up from the ranks and was the son of a fellah. I can see him in a skullcap and jellaba.'

'You forget I've been here before,' Violet reminded her husband.

In the customs shed Oliver was pestered by a travel agent called Gallal, who said he'd look after everything, the customs forms and so on, for six Egyptian pounds. It took a long time for the car to be unloaded from the ship, and then it had to be emptied of all the luggage for the customs inspection, which turned out to be cursory. Gallal was helpful with the filling in of forms concerning the car and the issuing of customs registration plates which had to be fixed over the British ones. Violet took no part in the proceedings. She allowed her husband to flap about and when they were ready to leave she sat in the passenger seat in the front of the Jaguar.

'Gallal is coming with us to a garage to get these wretched number plates fixed over ours and then to guide us on the right road to Cairo,' Oliver told his wife, who had pushed the seat back and was almost horizontal.

The Egyptian got into the back behind Oliver, having squeezed out of him a few more pounds. He had none of the charm of the immigration officer. He was a little man in a shiny blue suit and a cap with 'Gaby Tours' above the peak. During the fixing of the Egyptian number plates, the filling up with petrol and the drive to the outskirts of Alexandria, Violet was silent. After Gallal had set them on the road to Tanta, he got out quickly, asked for a pound which he didn't get and Oliver drove off.

'No ordinary Egyptian,' mumbled Violet.

'A tourist agency clerk on a minuscule salary. One can't blame him for trying to get as much as possible out of us.' Oliver glanced at his wife. She was asleep. He would have liked her to stay awake and tell him whether the road ahead was clear when he wanted to pass a truck or a clattering, swaying bus; with his steering wheel on the right it was difficult for him to see. But he didn't dare wake her. The road was cluttered with unruly traffic: overloaded lorries, buses bursting with passengers, carts drawn by water buffalo or camels, bikes and pedestrians and trotting donkeys. Progress was slow and it was nearly ten o'clock in the evening when they arrived at the Semiramis Hotel by the Nile in Cairo.

Violet was pleased with the spacious rooms of their suite. Their bedrooms were on either side of a sitting-room and each bedroom had a large bathroom.

'Thank heavens we're in an old-fashioned hotel,' remarked Oliver, 'and not in a modern one with box-like rooms and low ceilings. Are you going to unpack now?'

'I'll leave most of it till the morning. Let's have scrambled eggs sent up. I'm exhausted.'

'You slept well in the car,' said Oliver, pointedly.

'I had a wakeful night in that bobbing cork.'

☪

Ronald Wood's school, Nile College, provided accommodation in a modern block of flats. The only other occupant was Joan Webber. The flats had been built, albeit shoddily, for foreign teachers, who had fled, during the Suez campaign and now Ronald and Joan were the only two left. Their flats were on either side of a wide passage on the first floor. Both were basically furnished. Ronald, who spent most nights in the little apartment he had rented in Cairo, didn't mind the absence of comfort. Joan did. She persuaded the college bursar – who like many members of the staff found her charm, enhanced by her looks, hard to refuse – to provide her with tables, armchairs and a refrigerator. Ronald resented this favouritism, but not all that strongly, although he felt that being in a male-dominated society he should be given preference over her – and he'd been at the College a year longer than she.

Joan suggested that he should ask the bursar for similar treatment. He did. The bursar said he would do what he could, but it was difficult. Ronald knew that meant that nothing would be done and he'd have to put up with two upright chairs, a small, rickety table and a metal wardrobe decorated with Disney animals. He was one of the few people in the world who from an early age had detested Mickey Mouse, who, he thought, was an insult to mice, and as for Minnie!

Ronald did not feel at ease in such close proximity to a young woman. Joan was pleasant enough, and friendly, but all his life he had avoided the company of the female sex. He did not have anything to say to them, especially if they were young. Older women were different. He got on well with them, provided they had been properly educated. He did, though, prefer to be with men, those with similar tastes to his own.

Before Joan's arrival he had had the building to himself, and notwithstanding the fact that he only used his quarters twice a week, he liked it that way. Now that it was also occupied by Joan, he felt disconcerted.

Ronald had a little Fiat so did not have to use the train or the school bus when he went into Cairo. He sometimes gave Joan a lift. She never pressed him to give her one, but when he saw her walking to the station he offered her a ride, which she accepted demurely. She told him one day during the drive into Cairo about the Brents' imminent arrival.

'You know them?' Ronald said with surprise. 'I was at school with Oliver Brent. He's younger than I, but we were close friends. We've kept up, mostly by letter. He's a good correspondent. He wrote telling me that he and his wife were coming to Cairo. So you know them. What a coincidence!'

'I know her, Violet, better than Oliver.'

'I happened to be in England when they were married. I went to their wedding at Tring. I only saw her at the wedding. I gather she's rich. She certainly appeared so by the enormous house she had.'

'I know them well, or at least I know Violet well. She has oodles of money. What was the wedding like?'

'Not a grand affair at all. Only a handful of guests, including two ancient ladies, relations I suppose. One of them told me they lived on the estate. How did you meet the Brents?'

'At the theatre in London.'

Joan did not elaborate about the meeting. Ronald, though, having been told about Violet's sexual tastes by Oliver, wondered about his colleague.

☪

Joan was in the middle of a class when a servant brought her a message. It was from Violet, informing Joan of her arrival and asking her to contact her at the Semiramis. Joan put the piece of paper in her cardigan pocket and tried to continue the lesson.

'Love note?' inquired Mahmoud, the cheekiest and best-looking boy in the class.

The pupils burst into ribald laughter.

'Quiet!' commanded Joan, who hadn't learned to manage this disorderly bunch of early teenage boys and girls. She blushed and became flummoxed. 'Don't be silly, Mahmoud.'

The boy bristled, put on a fierce expression and, standing up, said, 'You call me silly?'

'Sit down, Mahmoud,' she ordered, adopting a stern regard; and to her relief, he did, smiling.

Joan liked her pupils. They did not harbour resentment when reprimanded. It was strange working in a country whose enemy was Britain almost as much as it was Israel. The army was trying to help the northern Yemenis capture Aden, and the British army was attempting to keep order until there could be proper elections. Not all the citizens of Aden and the southern Yemenis in the Hadramaut wanted to be dominated by the north. At the morning parade of the school, which Ronald skipped, the chief English teacher, Mr Thomas, a Copt, made announcements in English that sometimes included news from the Yemen. 'And at Aden,' Mr Thomas's deep, carefully enunciated voice announced, 'two British soldiers were killed yesterday. Sports Day with our sister school, Delta College in Alexandria, will take place on January 10th.' And then a girl's voice piped up with, 'The English winter ending in July, to begin again in August – Byron.' The third announcement amused Joan, who wondered if someone had searched through an anthology of English poets to find Anglophobic remarks, but Mr Thomas's words – and he was always so friendly – upset her. However, the news about the death of British soldiers at the hands of the insurgents (as the British called them) or the liberation forces (as the Arabs called them), Sports Day and Byron's famous saying drifted over the heads of the boys and girls of Nile College and did not seem to stir them. They did not listen to Mr Thomas's daily broadcasts; it required an effort for them to take in spoken English. Joan felt indignant and hurt. Brought up to believe that Britain was best, she no longer thought so, yet at the back of her mind, at the bottom of her heart, there existed a sentiment of patriotism that like a smouldering, newly-lit firework flared up when her country was derided or held in contempt. She felt angry after Mr Thomas's announcement. However, the fact that the pupils seemed oblivious to it calmed her; she admired the way they simply regarded her as Joan Webber, their teacher, who was trying to help them learn English. Joan came to the conclusion that their irritating misbehaviour in class was due to youthful exuberance and not directed at her because she was English.

☪

Ronald and Joan discussed the school, as teachers do: Mr Thomas, the headmaster, the students.

'You're right about the students,' Ronald said. 'They don't hate us. The Arabs possess the quality of differentiating between the British government and us. Unlike some people they do not take it out on us for the mistaken policies of our government. I was in the Lebanon at the time of the outrageous British and French invasion of Suez in 1956, and no animosity was shown towards me by the pupils of the Muslim school I was teaching at.'

'What about Mr Thomas? He seems to be anti-British. He made a crowing statement the other day about British soldiers being killed in Aden.'

'Mr Thomas has to toe the line. He is expected to make anti-British statements. It's the policy of the Ministry of Education, which has to follow the edicts of the Ministry of Infomation. There is, I'm sure, a spy from the government who reports on what goes on at the school, so Thomas has to pretend to support the regime, even if he doesn't really. If he spoke against it, he'd be sacked. Egypt is not a democracy, my dear. There's no real freedom of speech.'

'I realize that,' replied Joan. 'D'you think the spy listens outside my classroom to check that I'm not promoting British policy.'

'No. I don't think so.'

They were driving into town in Ronald's little car on their way to have lunch with Oliver and Violet at Groppi's.

'It's funny that you should know Oliver and I Violet,' remarked Joan.

'Violet's a lesbian,' said Ronald.

'I know *that*,' replied Joan, patly.

'But you're not a lesbian, are you?'

'No, but I did go to bed with Violet,' Joan confessed. 'Several times. I submitted out of curiosity and because of her relentless, tiger-like perseverance.'

'Oh dear,' said Ronald.

'She's attractive in the sense of being charming and interesting,' added Joan defensively. 'Having limitless money made her intriguing. She lives in a world I've never known, as different from my semi-attached home in Norbury as a Rolls is from your car.'

Ronald didn't like criticism of his Fiat; modest contraption though it was, he was proud of it. 'I see what you mean,' he consented grudgingly. 'I didn't realize you had lesbian tendencies.'

'I don't really. I applied for the job here because I was falling in love with a rich Thai, half Chinese. I needed to get away from him for a while, and also from Violet, who was becoming too possessive and presumptuous. Now Violet is here and Saman, whom I think I love, is in Hove.'

'I'd rather be here than in Hove, whatever the circumstances.'

After a pause, Joan asked, 'What about your sex life, Ronald? I know you're gay.'

'Is it obvious?' replied Ronald, somewhat disconcerted.

'Yes,' answered Joan, firmly and without hesitation. 'Do you have a boyfriend?'

'I do. His name is Khalid. He's not rich at all. If he were, he wouldn't turn me on.'

'You like to be in a superior position. That's rather imperialistic of you, Ronald.'

'I've never thought of my relationship with Khalid in that way. He's much younger than I, half my age in fact. I fear that his attraction to me is my having more money than he. He's not really queer.'

'I suppose in a way my relationship with Violet is not unlike yours with – what's his name again?'

'Khalid. You mean that Violet is me and you're Khalid? How absurd you are! What a ridiculous comparison! At least when it comes to going to bed there's no reluctance on Khalid's part. He doesn't need any pressurising in the form of "tiger-like perseverance."'

They were motoring along the right bank of the Nile and had just passed the Nilometer on the southern tip of Roda Island on the other side of the river.

Joan did not reply. Ronald was relieved that the subject of his and Joan's sex lives had lapsed. He had never had such an intimate conversation with a woman before. There was something about Joan, though, that made her seem different. Her natural acceptance of his being homosexual erased any embarrassment he would normally have had with a woman. He decided he liked her, but of course she could never be a kindred spirit.

'Did you know that that conical structure covers a well from the Fatimid era?' he asked.

Joan glanced back at the Nilometer. 'No. When was that?'

Ronald sighed. 'Tenth century. I find the antiquity of Egypt fascinating. Parts of this city are magical due to their connection with the past and the fact that they're still alive and still used.'

'You sound like a guide book.'

'Thank you.'

☪

Violet and Oliver had arrived at Groppi's. They were in the bar.

Violet rose, kissed Joan on both cheeks and then shook hands with Ronald.

'We met at your wedding,' Ronald reminded her.

'Of course,' said Violet. 'It's good to see you again.' Her tone suggested that she didn't remember him. 'Oliver is so pleased that you're here. What will you drink, Joan? And you, Mr Wood? We're having *zibib*.' She regained her chair. She was wearing a blue and brown patterned dress, a string of pearls, her wedding ring with her diamond engagement ring, and her father's signet ring on her right little finger. 'Come and sit by me, Joan.'

'No *zibib* for me, please,' said Joan. 'It tastes like medicine.'

'I find it delicious. I first had it when I was here in the war,' Violet informed everyone in the rather loud voice she adopted when she was nervous and excited. 'It's rather like Pernod or Berger Sec. It tastes a bit of aniseed or liquorice.'

'That's what I don't like about it,' said Joan. 'It's like taking a laxative.'

Violet laughed.

'It's more like ouzo or raki,' corrected Ronald. 'I'd like one, if I may.'

Violet addressed her husband, who was on his feet, hovering like a waiter by the table. 'Oliver, a *zibib* for Mr Wood—'

'Ronald, please.'

'For Ronald. And Joan?'

'A gin and orange, please.'

Oliver crossed to the bar. He didn't mince exactly, but his appearance in his impeccably cut grey suit and shining shoes and his slightly swishy gait made his tastes obvious to one, like Ronald, in the know. Oliver collected the drinks from the barman, who wore a tarboosh and a white shirt with a black bow-tie.

They wished each other good health.

Ronald turned to Oliver, while Violet talked animatedly to Joan.

Oliver leant forward, sitting on the edge of his chair. 'You may be able to help me,' he said to Ronald.

'Oh? How?'

Oliver glanced at his wife to see if she was still engaging Joan in her confidential chat. She was, so he continued, 'I have a friend here, an Egyptian. He works in a bank. I met him when I was doing my book.'

'How can I help?'

'I want to find him. He never replied to my letters, not even to remittances.'

'What's his name?'

'Khalid.'

'Khalid?' Ronald, astonished and indignant, exclaimed loudly, breaking the *sotto voce* they had tacitly fallen into.

Violet and Joan looked at the two men questioningly and returned to their own conversation.

'Yes, Khalid.'

'I know a Khalid. It couldn't be the same one, could it?'

Violet rose. 'Let's go into the restaurant.' She led the way, Oliver and Ronald following a few paces behind.

'Khalid what?' asked Oliver.

'Khalid Zeki,' said Ronald. 'Works in a bank, you say?'

'Yes.'

'Did you meet him in Ezbckich Gardens?'

'Yes,' admitted Oliver.

'So did I. It is the same chap. How funny!' Ronald didn't really feel it was funny at all.

'Are you in touch?' asked Oliver.

'Yes.'

'I see.'

'Hadn't we better join the others?'

Violet and Joan were already seated side by side on a banquette and in deep conversation.

On Ronald's advice they ordered the table d'hôte luncheon: *oeufs mayonnaise, riz financière, millefeuilles* and a carafe of red Egyptian wine. During the meal Violet and Joan continued their tête-à-tête, ignoring the two men, who went on talking about Khalid. They were jealous of each other.

'It's most extraordinary in this big city,' said Oliver, 'that we should know the same person. How long have you known him?'

'Just over a year. I met him soon after I came to teach at Nile College.'

'And you picked him up in Ezbekieh Gardens?'

'Yes.'

'Like me when I was working on my book, a few years ago.'

'Would you like me to tell him you're here?' asked Ronald, generously.

'Yes,' replied Oliver. 'But he should know that I was coming. I wrote to him giving him a rough date.'

'I'm seeing him this evening.'

'Where?'

'In my flat. I have a flat just off Tahrir Square.'

'Could I join you?' asked Oliver.

'I think it's better if I see him alone first.'

'I understand.'

'What are you two muttering about?' inquired Violet. 'You sound most conspiratorial.'

Oliver countered, 'I thought you did too.'

'We were discussing a trip to Luxor and Aswan over Christmas, when Joan is free.'

Through the door came Cedric. He frowned when he saw Ronald and the others. He came up to their table. Oliver rose and they shook hands and he introduced him to Violet. Ronald introduced him to Joan.

'Won't you join us?' said Violet, assuming the role of hostess.

A chair was brought and Cedric sat between Ronald and Oliver.

'I much enjoyed *Among the Minarets* and *Blatant Folly*,' lied Cedric to Oliver.

'Good of you to say so,' said Oliver. '*Blatant Folly* was a complete flop, like many second books. Can't give it away now.' He laughed.

'Are you a resident in Cairo?' asked Violet of Cedric in the tone of one who feels she ought to say something to the new arrival, but really had no interest in what the reply would be.

'I work on the local English newspaper.'
'So you live here.'
'I have small flat in Kasr-el-Nil Street, near Liberation Square.'
'I remember Kasr-el-Nil. It runs from the great square that used to be called Ismael Square to the Place de l'Opera, doesn't it?'
'Yes,' said Ronald. 'And Suleiman Pasha, the main drag, is now called Talaat Harb after the founder of Bank Misr, the Bank of Egypt. Suleiman was French. He became a Muslim and was made a pasha by Ismael. The Nasser government, not liking the principal street of the capital called after a foreigner, renamed it Talaat Harb, but everyone still calls it Suleiman Pasha. The statue outside Groppi's used to be that of Suleiman Pasha; it was replaced by one of the banker in 1964.'
'Ronald's writing a guide book about Cairo,' teased Joan.
'Are you really?' asked Violet, interested.
'No.'

☪

Ronald's Cairo flat was hardly worthy of the name. At the top of an apartment building owned by an Armenian, it consisted of a bedroom, a kitchen-bathroom, and a terrace that looked across the city at the bare Makattam hills. A lift with glass sides ascended to the third floor, and then a steep flight of stairs led up to the flat, which was just under the roof. The building dated from before the First World War and was in a rather dilapidated state: the lift was unreliable and the banisters were unsteady. It was pretty miserable accommodation, less than basic, and having the gas cooker close to the bath seemed a somewhat dangerous arrangement; however, the place was cheap and central. Ronald liked the terrace. A burly, genial Sudanese *bawab* in a white skull cap and billowing jellaba was on duty at the entrance.

On the evening of the lunch party at Groppi's, Khalid, as arranged, arrived at the flat punctually at six.

'Hello, Mister Ron,' Khalid cried cheerfully when Ronald opened the door.

They sat on upright chairs by a small rough table in what Ronald called the sitting area of the room. On the table were six oranges and six bananas, which Ronald had bought in preparation for the visit.

'A beer, Khalid?'

'No, Coca,' demanded the young Egyptian as he began to devour the fruit like a hungry elephant, except that he did peel the oranges and the bananas, or rather tore them open, not using the knife provided. Ronald had often wondered about this penchant for fruit. It could hardly act as an aphrodisiac. He had never asked his friend why he wished to consume so much fruit before sex; perhaps Khalid thought it acted as an prophylactic. Ronald didn't mind Khalid's voraciousness; one forgives a lover for gobbling. Besides, he loved Khalid in a way; at least he depended on him for a weekly and sometimes bi-weekly outlet. He decided to put off broaching the subject of Oliver until afterwards.

'Afterwards' meant after the bed and after the bath. It disconcerted Ronald that Khalid spent more time in the latter than in the former. When, at last, Khalid emerged from the bathroom, he sat again at the rickety table and accepted Ronald's offer of a beer. He was wearing one of the suits made out of cloth that Ronald had given him, the charcoal-grey cloth chosen because it was thought to be suitable for a bank clerk. The young man wore no tie, but looked spruce and shining after the bath; his dark-brown frizzled hair was closely cropped.

Ronald took a swig of Egyptian brandy and said, 'I met a friend of yours today.'

Khalid frowned. 'Friend? Who?'

'An Englishman called Oliver Brent.'

The frowned deepened.

'Do you know him?'

'Who?'

'Oliver Brent. A short fat man with a red face and greying hair.'

Khalid hesitated.

'You know him?' Ronald reiterated.

'Mister Olli?' Khalid blushed.
'Yes, that would be him. Where did you meet him?'
'In Cairo.'
'When?'
'Before two, three year.'
'He writes to you?'
'Yes.'
'You write to him?'
'No.'
'He send you money?'
'Yes.'
'You love him?'
'He good man.'
'I see.' Ronald pursed his lips for a moment. 'He wants to see you. He's staying at the Semiramis. You want to see him?'
'Yes, I mus'.'
Ronald guessed that Khalid had received Oliver's letter and knew he was at the Semiramis, but he did not challenge the young man about this. 'His wife is with him.'
'He have wife?'
'Yes.'
'He not say he have wife.'
'No?'
The two fell into silence. Ronald finished his brandy and Khalid his beer.
'You not mind Mister Olli?' asked Khalid.
'Not at all,' Ronald lied, knowing he sounded as if he did mind. 'You met him before me.'
'I love you, Mister Ron.'
'And Mister Olli? You love him?'
'He good man. He kind to me.'
Another pause.
'Let's go and eat.'
'Where we go, Mister Ron?'
'Not to the Semiramis. To the Matham-el-Jeish.'
'OK, Mister Ron.'
The army restaurant, so named, was nearby. It served kebab with round, flat Arab bread.
No further mention was made of 'Mister Olli'.

☪

Notwithstanding the uneasy truce with Israel, the shaky Egyptian economy and the skirmishes against the British army in Aden, life in Cairo, to a foreign visitor at least, carried on with reasonable smoothness. The visiting foreigner or average tourist was able to lead a comfortable existence since he could exclude himself from the dire problems that confronted Egypt; after all they weren't his problems; the critical situation did not directly concern him. He was unaware of the struggle that most Egyptians had to make to survive. It was their irrepressible sense of humour, their natural jolliness, that concealed their wretched living conditions, which had little chance of improvement in spite of promises from the government that projects such as the creation of Liberation province, Lake Nasser and its dam, and the prospect of oil being discovered off the Red Sea and Mediterranean coasts would bring about prosperity. It was their unshakeable belief in Islam that kept up the morale of most Egyptians. *Allahu Akbar* ('God is Great') they would cry, and Allah, they staunchly believed, would save them from disaster; and there was Nasser, their leader, in whom they had implicit faith. Unlike the average visitor, Ronald knew all this and he admired the philosophy of the Egyptian man-in-the-street.

After giving Khalid a length of cloth, Ronald, obtusely, wondered why the young man didn't have it made up; at last Ronald gathered through indirect hints that Khalid couldn't afford to pay the tailor's bill. When Ronald paid it Khalid was touchingly grateful. This incident brought home to Ronald Khalid's borderline existence. He did not blame him for accepting aid from Oliver, or from him when after a session he gave him a few pounds.

Ronald was naturally jealous of Oliver – who isn't envious when someone richer than oneself comes along and turns out to be a rival? It worried Ronald that Khalid had this connection with Oliver. He had been happy to have a regular friend who put an end to his promiscuity. Khalid, sturdy, good-looking, presentable, was just the friend he had always wanted. To have the affair upset was hard to bear. He did not like the idea of sharing Khalid with Oliver.

☪

Although Violet outwardly appeared a mild, withdrawing person, she was in fact a determined and forceful one. Her father had spoilt her but at the same time had been a severe parent, remote and strict. She had been afraid of him. He would indulge her whims and then suddenly become forbidding, as if his indulgence would be taken as weakness. Violet had inherited these characteristics in a milder form; in her relationship with her husband she practised them. She bought Oliver a Jaguar, which he had pined for, and then showed that it really belonged to her by registering and insuring it in her name, so that Oliver did not feel it was his. Violet's father owed his outstanding success in business to his knack of seeming to be malleable and then suddenly becoming ruthless. It was Violet's quiet powers of persuasion that had gained Joan's and Saman's presence at Le Caprice after the theatre, and enticed Joan to Tring and into her bed.

Joan's life at Nile College compared with that at the language school at Hove was at first exciting and exhilarating; she soon, however, began to feel bored and frustrated. Ronald had been polite and helpful, but he remained aloof, and spent most nights in Cairo. After school he would drive off, and return the next day for his first lesson, which did not necessarily coincide with the first class of the day.

In the intimate conversation Joan had had in Ronald's car on the way to meet the Brents at Groppi's, she had omitted to tell him about Adnan, the maths teacher at Nile College, not that there was much to tell. Unlike most members of the staff, Adnan was a bachelor. He had the confidence of a man who knows he is good-looking. Soon after her arrival he started showing an interest in her; once he suggested he pay a visit to her flat. She turned down the offer firmly. After her rebuff

Adnan did not do more than give her soulful, longing looks, which embarrassed Joan.

Young men like Adnan didn't have girlfriends. They found relief in cheap brothels, and their parents would press them to marry. Some Egyptian men had a secret liaison with a married woman. Such an arrangement did not appeal to Adnan because of its dangers, its expense and because he was not attracted to the middle-aged. It was possible, Adnan knew, to meet a European or American widow or divorcee in one of the tourist hotels who would be delighted to invite him to dinner and then to her bedroom. Adnan was no gigolo. Joan was his ideal. It was sad that she would not respond to his advances and that he had no money to back them up.

Although Joan had taken the job at Nile College to get away from the clutches of Violet and the allure of Saman, she was pleased that the Brents had come to Egypt. Their arrival meant that there were friends to see in Cairo. Ronald was amicable but was no companion. She was lonely.

☪

On the day after the luncheon party at Groppi's, Ronald stayed later than usual in his flat at Nile College. He had a pile of exercise books to correct; he did not like to do school work in his downtown hideout. Around six o'clock in the evening he and Joan left their separate flats simultaneously, to their mutual surprise. Ronald had shut his door carefully and started towards the stairs on tiptoe. He had been embarrassed by Joan's sudden appearance and hoped she had not noticed his creeping exit.

'Going into town, Joan?'

'Yes.'

'May I give you a lift?' Ronald didn't want to; he felt he had to make the offer.

'That would be very kind. Could you drop me off at the Semiramis?'

'With pleasure. Are you going to see the Brents?'

'Yes.'

On the way into town, Ronald asked, 'Do you think you're going to like it here, Joan?'

'I'm not sure. The work is pretty awful. Do you enjoy it?'

'No, but I enjoy Cairo. I regard the job as a means to be able to stay here. Teaching is sheer hell. I divide my life into two compartments: the school, which I endure, and my private life, which I enjoy.'

'You're lucky to have a sort of separate existence. I have only one: the school. It is not enough. I feel frustrated.'

'Perhaps the Brents will help.'

'Perhaps they will. I'm not absolutely sure that I want them to.'

Just as Ronald was depositing Joan outside the Semiramis, he saw Khalid's back receding into the hotel. He controlled his urge to call out to his friend and drove off feeling jealous and unhappy.

☪

Joan and Khalid were, apart from the lift boy in baggy blue trousers, a short gold-braided jacket and a tarboosh, the only passengers to the third floor, where the Brents had their suite. During their ascent, Khalid furtively shot a few concupiscent glances at Joan, who was conservatively garbed in a dress and a cardigan. The dark lift boy grinned. Joan frowned and looked down. On arrival the two visitors found they were going in the same direction. As they were approaching Suite 363, the door opened and Violet and Oliver appeared. Like a rabid vulture, Violet swooped upon Joan, grabbed her by the arm and pulled her into the sitting-room and thence into her bedroom; Oliver less violently hustled Khalid into the sitting-room and invited him to take a seat, which he did on an upright French-style chair. Oliver sat on the *chaise-longue*.

'It's very good to see you, Khalid, after so long,' said Oliver.

'Not at all, Mister Olli.'

'What would you like to drink? It's after six. Time for something, what? I have some whisky. Do you like whisky? I can ring down for beer if you'd prefer it.'

'I like whisky.'

'Good.' Oliver rose and went to the sideboard. 'There's no ice. I forgot to order ice. Would you like some ice? I could have some brought up.'

'Just whisky all right.'

'Good.' Oliver realized that Khalid's English, both in vocabulary and in comprehension, was limited, so he carefully articulated his words and spoke loudly; he sounded as if he were giving dictation to a backward class. At the sideboard, while pouring out liberal measures of whisky, he said, 'It is a long time since we met. It must be three years.' He handed Khalid a glass and sat again on the *chaise-longue*.

'Well, good luck.' He raised his glass. Khalid did the same. Oliver sipped; Khalid took a swig.

'What do you say in Arabic when you drink?'

'We say "*sahat cum*".'

'What does that mean?'

'It mean "health", your health.'

'We say much the same.' Oliver took another sip; Khalid drained his glass.

'Have another whisky?'

'No thanks, Mister Olli.'

Oliver smiled. He was excited by Khalid's presence; he wondered how he was going to get him into the bedroom.

'Would you like a bath?'

'Pardon?'

'I have a very nice *hammam*. Would you like to have a *hammam*?'

'No thanks.'

'Oh.'

Silence reigned for a while. Khalid jogged his right knee.

'My bedroom is through that door.' Oliver jerked his head in the direction of his bedroom. 'Would you like to see it?' Khalid did not reply.

Oliver emptied his glass and, emboldened by the whisky, rose and took hold of one of Khalid's hands. 'Come, let me show you my bedroom.'

'Who those ladies?' asked Khalid, not rising.

'Oh, don't bother about them. They won't come in here. They have women's business to discuss: dresses, clothes, that sort of thing. Come on.' Oliver was surprised at his own bravura. He still held Khalid's hand. He gave it a tug.

Khalid got up and Oliver guided him into the bedroom, which was furnished with two armchairs, a chest of drawers, a dressing table and a high double bed with iron bars at the head and foot and each corner crowned with a brass bauble. Oliver locked the door, turned and was pleased to see that Khalid had already taken off his pullover. The older man advanced, flung his arms round the young Egyptian and tried to kiss him, but Khalid moved his head and the lips only brushed his cheek. Oliver put a hand on Khalid's crotch and was pleased to feel a stiff prick. They undressed at speed and were soon naked on the bed. Khalid pushed Oliver on to his stomach. Oliver groaned. He would have liked a slower approach, a coaxing, a fondling before being forced to yield. Khalid was rather a selfish lover. However, he did wait until Oliver had turned on his side and masturbated before leaping out of the bed.

'You say you have bath, Mister Olli?'

'Yes,' replied Oliver, not really fulfilled 'through that door.' Oliver lay back in the old-fashioned bed. In the day-dreams of sex with Khalid he had had at Tring, there had been more co-operation.

☪

Violet and Joan sat opposite each other in the armchairs at the foot of the double bed, identical to the one in Oliver's room. The two women were shy of one another. Joan told Violet about Nile College: the mischievous pupils, Mr Thomas, the Coptic English teacher, the remote headmaster, the plain fare in the school dining-hall, and Ronald Wood. She did not mention Adnan.

'It sounds perfectly awful,' said Violet. 'So dull. And you spend all your evenings all alone in that frightful flat you describe? What about Ronald?'

'He spends most nights in his flat in Cairo; anyway he's not interested in the company of women.'

'And the Egyptian women on the staff, are they not friendly?'

'They're friendly enough, but they have their own lives to lead. Most of them are married and mothers.'

'How long are you going to stand it?'

'Stand what?'

'Being at that ghastly school.'

'My contract is for one year, but it's renewable. I don't think I'll ask for a renewal.'

'And then what?'

'I shall go back to England and see about another job.' She thought of Saman, but did not mention him.

'Why don't you resign now? I would look after you.'

'I don't want to let them down,' said Joan, dutifully.

'Why not? They pay you nothing.'

'I can manage. I don't need much,' went on Joan, stoically.

'I'll give you an allowance,' announced Violet.

'No. I must look after myself.'

Violet rose and went over to Joan. She put out a hand and stroked the young woman's hair. 'I'm very fond of you, Joan. You know that. Resign and stay with me.'

'What about Oliver?'

'He doesn't mind what I do, what arrangements I make. He has his boyfriends.'

'I must say,' remarked Joan, recoiling a little from Violet's hand, which was now stroking the back of her neck, 'yours is the strangest of marriages.'

'We, Oliver and I, get on very well. We go our own different ways. It suits us. We may tease each other but we don't quarrel about our private friends.' Violet dropped to her knees and slipped a hand down the top of Joan's dress and squeezed a nipple. 'I'll look after you, darling,' she said soothingly. 'You need have no worries, financial or otherwise, if you stay with me. We could have a perfect time, my pet.' Violet kissed Joan on the lips; her other hand grasped Joan's thigh. 'Come, let's make love. I've been longing for you.'

Joan no longer resisted. She meekly allowed Violet to undress her, and obeyed her command to lie on the bed; after all it was not the first time she had consented to make love with Violet.

'You look so beautiful lying there like that,' said Violet, taking off her clothes.

☪

Violet and Oliver were in the sitting-room of their suite in the Semiramis Hotel. Their respective paramours had gone. Violet was in one of her bossy, planning moods brought on, Oliver guessed, by her feeling of guilt about sex. Oliver had no compunction about his session with Khalid; although it wasn't very satisfactory, he felt content and was looking forward to dinner. He sipped his whisky.

'We must get things down on paper,' said Violet, a trifle grimly.

'What sort of things?' asked Oliver, dreamily.

'About what we are going to do here.'

'I thought you had just done what you set out to do.'

'Please don't be facetious, Oliver. What I mean is I don't want the days to drift by so that at the end of our stay, we've done nothing.'

'There's no danger of that, is there? We've both been here before. We've seen most of the sights, but there isn't one that isn't worth seeing again. I suggest you draw up plans, on paper of course, for a thorough revisiting of places. Anyway, you said something about going to Luxor with Joan Webber.'

'Yes. We must talk about that.'

'Webber,' mused Oliver. 'There was a master at school called Webber. He taught maths and commanded the school corps. I never liked the name. I didn't like him. He was a little man with a squashed-up face, lined like a map and—'

'Don't digress,' interrupted Violet peevishly. 'First, we must arrange the Luxor trip. You'll come, of course. We'll go by car, down the Red Sea coast and then inland to Luxor.'

'I believe there are some good hotels now on the coast,' said Oliver.

'In Luxor we'll stay at the Winter Palace.'

'If we can get in.'

'We can't stay there if it's full.'

'Perhaps it won't be. I'll ask Khalid to come with us. He'd help us as a guide. The trouble about booking is that if we go by car we won't know the exact date of our arrival.' Oliver rose. 'Let's go and eat, darling. I'm hungry.' The endearment had become automatic; sometimes he used it in front of married couples to show that they led an ordinary matrimonial existence.

'I don't want to eat in the hotel. The food seems tired somehow.'

'Groppi's?'

'Groppi's is all right for lunch, not for dinner.'

'I know,' said Oliver, suddenly inspired. 'We'll go to Sofar. We can walk, there.'

It was a fine evening, clement, balmy almost, and the streets were not crowded; there was a leisurely atmosphere. People strolled rather than hastened. Egyptian eyes examined the English couple as they made their way to Restaurant Sofar. The large, striding foreign woman and the scuttling fat man must have seemed a quaint sight.

Violet and Oliver had onion soup followed by chicken-liver risotto, with which they had a bottle of Château Gianaclis, an Egyptian red wine, which Violet declared to be barely drinkable. She drank half a glass; Oliver finished the bottle.

☪

In the early evening Ronald was wont to take a preprandial stroll round the streets of the Khedive Ismael's quarter of Cairo. Modern at the end of the nineteenth century, its buildings were now sadly run-down; to Ronald, though, they were infinitely more appealing than the high-rise constructions that were slowly beginning to ascend here and there. Seedy, perhaps, the quarter was not alien or unfriendly; on the contrary it was, like its inhabitants, dignified and warm. He walked up Suleiman Pasha and then Sarwat Pasha to the Opera House and Ezbekich Gardens, outside which were bookstalls lit by pressure lamps. He browsed through the English and French books on sale and, finding nothing he wished to buy, dropped into a small bookshop on his way back which had an attraction not connected with literature. In attendance at the shop was a saucy lad in a skullcap and jellaba, under which he wore nothing else. The owner of the shop would usually be at the back behind a bookcase, lying on an empty shelf. Should there be a customer who actually wanted to buy a book, the lad would shout to the owner, who, with a querulous groan, would descend from his horizontal position and appear. He was about forty, had sleek black hair, parted in the middle, and wore a dark-blue suit that had seen better days. The lad's experienced eye could discern whether the person was a bibliophile or a voyeur. If the former he would adopt a studious regard, furrowing his eyebrows; if the latter he would beckon with his head, go behind a bookshelf, raise his jellaba with his left hand, and with his right waggle his impressive organ and grin lasciviously. Any attempt by the visitor to help would cause the garment to drop and the thumb of the lad's right hand to rub the forefinger. A nod from the visitor would bring up the jellaba again and his hand would take over; the resulting spurt shot on to a row of books; the proffered banknote was snatched and made to disappear with a conjuror's sleight; the visitor would then leave the shop in haste. On one occasion for Ronald, who sometimes helped spray the books, the lad bent over, his jellaba round his shoulders, but delectable though the sight was, Ronald demurred and attended to the front.

When Ronald entered the shop that evening there was a scuffle and Cedric bolted out of the door as if he were being chased. He did not seem to notice Ronald, who then took over and finished off what his friend had begun.

☪

Cedric's parents divorced when their only child was at school. Much to Cedric's regret his mother could not afford to send him to university. She told him that on leaving school he must get a job. He found one in the book department of a London store. He lived with his mother in Putney. When war broke out in September 1939 he tried to join one of the forces, but was turned down because of his bad eyesight. He managed to get employment on a local newspaper in Brighton. He did not enjoy the work but stuck it out until the middle of the war, when he landed a job on the *Baghdad Times* through the help of a friend in the Information Department of the Foreign Office. Cedric did not like Baghdad: the pay was poor and the accommodation basic. He put up with a cell of a room at the YMCA, institutional food and an irregular supply of hot water. The other inmates were teachers from Britain who, like him, were unfit for active service, plus two sergeants and three corporals from the RAF base at Habbaniya attached to the British Embassy, an English telephone engineer working for the Iraqi government, and two British oil engineers under contract to the Iraq Petroleum Company. Like the Anglo-Iranian Oil Company in Abadan, the IPC was British-run.

The YMCA was managed by a Mr Lampard and his wife. Lampard was a big man with a shock of white hair, a loud voice, a sallow complexion and dark eyes. He wore a khaki outfit consisting of a bush shirt and trousers, as if he wished to seem like an officer, but his general appearance was Levantine; his wife, mouse-like, was English, an ineffectual woman who, when a lodger complained to her about some matter, would say, 'I'll ask Mr Lampard.' Cedric never bothered to find out anything about the background of the Lampards. He did notice, however, that once a week the manager would go off in his capacious shooting-brake and return the next day with a full load of cardboard boxes containing Cedric knew not what.

Cedric was incurious by nature, and although a journalist he, being lazy, was not one to make an effort to dig up information. Nevertheless he was good at collating news reports and summarizing them into long or short columns in the newspaper – at school he had been good at that important exercise: précis. Occasionally, the editor, a blunt Scotsman, told him to write a leading article. This caused Cedric much anguish as he had great difficulty in finding anything to say; he didn't know very much or care a lot about the situation in Iraq. He was a neutral person. He did sympathise with the Palestinians in 1948 when Israel was created, but he also felt sorry for the Jews in Europe who had nowhere to go.

Social life in Baghdad was limited for an undistinguished journalist. Cedric was not one who liked parties. He joined the Alwiyah Club but did not participate in its activities. He was gauche with women, not really understanding them or liking them. Several of the wives of British officials or businessmen tried, out of kindness, to get Cedric to attend their cocktail or dinner parties. Fortunately, he was able to excuse himself from going to these expat social functions, to which no Iraqis were invited, by claiming he was on duty at the paper.

Cedric was tallish, slender; his brown hair had from the age of twenty-five started to become sparse, and his brown eyes squinted through spectacles. He was not a mother's choice for her daughter, or even that of a desperate English spinster.

When Cedric masturbated men came into his mind rather than women. He tried to think of a naked woman but she soon dissolved cinematically into Adam, the Chaldean barman at the Club, a handsome young man with a fetching smile, who, Cedric thought, liked him. Cedric's diffidence prevented him from making an approach and he merely lusted after him; in order to stay in Adam's presence he would drink more than he wanted to and tip him generously, although members were not supposed to tip Club servants. One evening on his return from the Club he submitted to the insistent and lubricious advances of the nightwatchman at the YMCA, and bent over behind a bush in the garden. Afterwards Cedric was ashamed of allowing the far-from-attractive guardian, who was at least fifteen years older than him and looked more, to play the masculine role. He did not permit the watchman, wretchedly attired in keffiyeh, cotton *dishdasha* and discarded army overcoat, and bearing an antiquated rifle over his shoulder, to repeat the performance, in spite of frequent requests which Cedric warded off with a banknote. This humiliating lapse caused Cedric to apply for accommodation at the Club, which after a few months he obtained.

Living at the Club was much better than existing at the YMCA. He had two rooms and a bathroom instead of a tiny cell; there was a swimming pool, and the food was an improvement on Mrs Lampard's run-of-the-mill menus; it was a relief not to have to listen to Lampard holding forth at the head of the table with his napkin tucked into his shirt collar. The manager of the Club was a decent fellow, decent and affable. The drawback of being at the Club was the proximity of Adam, which disturbed Cedric.

In 1952 Baghdad erupted into riots. Colleges and schools closed. Students demonstrated. In a way the Iraqis were emulating what had occurred in Egypt when King Farouk was ousted and Gamal Abdel Nasser became president of what was called the United Arab Republic. The cause of these upheavals was mainly the policies of the Western powers, above all Britain and the USA, whom the Arabs felt were trying to continue their imperialistic control. The creation of Israel in 1948, although a result of years of planning and struggle by the Jews both inside and outside Palestine, was considered to be a Western plot to dominate the Middle East.

The riots in Baghdad lasted three days: pro-Western businesses and Western embassies (in particular the British Embassy) were threatened and had to be protected by the Iraqi army. The premises of the *Baghdad Times* were stormed by a rampaging mob; Cedric, the editor and the other employees had to escape out of the back door. After the riots the centre of the city looked as if it had been captured; the atmosphere was of a place that had been defeated; the crew of an army tank parked at the head of Rashid Street resembled victors ashamed of their victory; there was no triumph on their faces.

At the Club there was much speculation about the future. The majority of the members, most of them British, was on the side of the pro-Western government. Cedric decided that he had had enough of Iraq and more than enough of what to him were the ignorant, wrong-minded British residents. Privately he found he was on the side of the rioters and the students who supported them. This minor insurrection changed Cedric's attitude, and his former indifference to the situation was substituted by a strong pro Arab stance. One of the things that impressed him about the rioters was that when they sacked a Western-owned travel agency they smashed open the safe but did not take any of the money it contained.

At the Club bar he fell into conversation with a visiting British journalist, who had been sent to Baghdad by his London paper to cover the troubles in Iraq. The journalist, Peter Bakewell by name, was in favour of Nasser and approved of Cedric's sympathy with the rioters; they both agreed that Britain and the USA had given the Arabs a raw deal. Bakewell, who lived in Cairo, told Cedric that there was a vacancy on the *Egyptian Mail*, and suggested that he apply for it. 'The job is badly paid,' he warned, 'but Cairo is a damned sight more interesting than here, more amusing and, above all, it's not subservient to the West.' In a few months Cedric left for Cairo and took up the job on the *Egyptian Mail*. He left Iraq with few regrets. Adam was one of them, but only until the eve of his departure, when, after several whiskies, he made a pass at him in the bar lavatory and was firmly rebuffed. The rebuff made him leave Iraq without any regrets at all.

In Cairo Cedric first stayed at the Green Valley Hotel in Sharia Sarwat Pasha, a street that was not renamed as nothing could be found against the pasha, a mild and worthy patriotic statesman. The manager of the Green Valley was an Italian-Egyptian named Roberto, bald, genial and rotund, and proud of the fact that his wife sang in the chorus of the Cairo Opera

Company. The hotel began on the third floor and the rooms were spacious and fairly quiet. Cedric settled into the hotel and would have stayed indefinitely if a colleague on the *Egyptian Mail* had not persuaded him to move into a flat that had just fallen vacant, owing to the sudden departure of a Syrian doctor. The flat was small but very central, being in a block next the Metro Cinema, just off Tahrir Square. In his hasty and unexplained flight the doctor had left behind his medical books, which Cedric did not disturb from the bookcase in the little sitting room. Far from ideal, the flat looked onto the well of the building and therefore had only an inside view; the main advantage was that the rent was low and controlled and could not be raised by a rapacious landlord.

Cedric had learnt the rudiments of Arabic in Baghdad. In Cairo he applied himself more seriously to the language, and by 1965, when he met Ronald Wood, who took up his teaching post at Nile College in that year, he was quite fluent and could decipher the Arabic script.

☪

Joan was in a quandary. She wished she hadn't given way to Violet's blandishments. It was hard, though, to resist the older woman's persuasive powers. In England she had been attracted by Violet's style of living. Violet's wealth oiled the wheels of her and Oliver's lives to such an extent that the couple seemed to have no worries at all. For them life was devoid of impediments; they appeared to have no problems. For Joan such an existence was enviable. She had always had to work hard. Her parents had helped her when, at university, she had been short of funds, but not willingly; she had had to beg for cash. In Hove, she had envied Saman's carefree manner; and then Violet had come into her life.

Joan received a letter from the Thai informing her of his imminent arrival. What was she to do? She dreaded his coming, and yet she knew she would be pleased to see him. And he was flying all the way from London to see her: she was sure he wasn't in the least interested in the sights of Egypt. And then there was Adnan at the school. She knew from the wistful looks he gave her that he still hoped she would succumb to his charms, in spite of the rebuff she had given him. She was beginning to find his presence bothersome. She had left England to eschew further entanglement with Violet and Saman; now the mesh of the net seemed finer than ever.

☪

'You simply can't,' Oliver said to Violet. 'Why bring this up again? We've discussed it before.'

'I have no qualms about going,' countered Violet.

They were in the sitting room of their suite at the Semiramis. Violet had reiterated her intention to drive to Luxor alone with Joan.

'For two Western women to careen about Egypt in an expensive car is sheer madness. You would be prey to thieves, robbers, rapists and thugs. Why don't you fly to Luxor, stay in the Winter Palace and employ a guide?'

'I see your ruse.'

'What do you mean?'

'You want the car to take your friend on a trip.'

'How did you guess?' Oliver smiled.

'My dear Oliver, d'you think that after ten years of marriage, or a sort of marriage, I don't know what goes on in your mind?'

'That's rather frightening. I didn't know I had a mind-reader for a wife.'

'You're transparent.'

Oliver bridled. 'Oh, never mind about that. We have no secrets, do we? But seriously, Violet, I do think it would be the height of folly for you and Joan to motor alone, without even a driver, to Luxor.'

'You could come with us, Oliver, and bring your friend.'

'Khalid works in a bank. He can't get the time off, not more than two or three days.'

'Where were you thinking of going with him?'

'To Fayoum.'

'Oh, so you've planned it already.'

'Not really. Will you promise me, Violet, that you'll give up the idea of motoring with Joan to Luxor?'

'No. I won't promise anything. I will think about it.' With a sigh, Oliver rose and went into his bedroom.

☪

'To tell you the truth, Cedric,' Ronald said to his journalist friend, 'I wish the Brents hadn't come here. Oliver met Khalid before I did, when he was writing his *magnum opus*, and Khalid has been to see him. He feels he has to, as Oliver sends him money.'

'The Brents won't be staying here forever, will they?' returned Cedric. 'They're not thinking of taking up residence, are they? You'll be able to exercise your *droit de seigneur* when they've gone.'

The two friends were at one of their regular luncheon meetings in Groppi's. Cedric was having his habitual omelette and Ronald *loup de mer*, the main dish on the table d'hôte menu.

'They, the Brents,' went on Ronald, 'are wreckers. They are the kind of people who get a kick out of destroying other people's affairs, And what's more—'

'Don't tell me there's more.'

'Yes, there is,' insisted Ronald. 'There's Joan Webber.'

'What has she got to do with it?'

'She's being chased by Violet Brent.'

'How do you know? You told me you hardly ever spoke to her, misogynist that you are.'

'I gave her a lift to the Semiramis and she said something about Violet being in love with her. Also, there's a Thai in her life, but she didn't say much about him. Just as Oliver is trying to estrange Khalid from me, so Violet is out to make Joan give up her Thai. That is what I surmise.'

Cedric's omelette arrived. He examined it rather disdainfully before picking up his knife and fork. After a mouthful, he said, 'The trivial liaisons of the Brents and, if you don't mind my saying so, of yours and Joan's – is it Joan?' Ronald nodded, 'are of scant interest to me. They are of no importance at all. What is important is the situation in the Yemen. As you know, Egypt has sent troops there to assist the Marxist National Liberation Front.'

'Backed by the Soviet Union, I suppose. I didn't know Egypt was supporting the Marxists. Where do they come from?'

'They're what the British call terrorists,' explained Cedric, 'and the Egyptians freedom fighters. The government in Sana'a is pro-Western but they want to take over Aden and the South. The British want Aden and the Protectorate, South Yemen, to become independent; in fact they've promised independence in 1968 to what they call the Federation of South Arabia and Aden.'

'The whole thing seems like a typical post-colonial balls-up,' said Ronald. 'Or one might call it a patent trick to control South Arabia. What exactly is the British army doing in Aden?'

'Trying to protect the port from the terrorists.'

'Or as you, Cedric, would say, the freedom fighters.'

'Quite.'

'Your paper doesn't say much, if anything, about the campaign in the Yemen.'

'Sometimes it's necessary not to reveal what precisely is going on,' admitted Cedric.

'So you're in favour of censorship. I'm dead against it. I'm in favour of openness.'

'In all matters?'

'Yes,' answered Ronald, raising his voice.

'In private matters?' Cedric gave a sardonic smile.

'Well, no, that's different.'

The two friends finished their meal in silence. Cedric rose first, nodded, and left for the *Egyptian Mail*. Ronald waited a few minutes and then drove to his miserable hutch off Tahrir Square.

☪

Saman had arrived in Cairo and checked into the Hilton Hotel on the Corniche, as the road on the right bank of the Nile was now called. It was early evening, the cocktail hour. He went into the bar and ordered a beer from the barman, a swarthy Egyptian in a white jacket and black bow tie. The barman wore his tarboosh at a raffish angle, and a pencil-thin moustache graced his upper lip. Saman asked him if he knew of Nile College and was informed that it was about 15 kilometres south of the capital.

'How I go there?' he asked.

The barman told him there was a train from Bab-el-Louk Station, which was up a street off Tahrir Square, and just past the American University.

Saman decided to walk to the station to find out where it was exactly; he would go to Nile College the next day. Around the entrance to the hotel, which gave on to Tahrir Square, Saman was pestered by pimps and touts. He ignored them and hastened his step. About half of the male pedestrians were clothed in skullcaps and jellabas, the other half in trousers and open-necked shirts, with jackets or pullovers. It was fresh rather than cold. The women in black *abbayas* outnumbered those in Western garb. The atmosphere was not hostile, but to Saman it was alien. The dark examining eyes that darted at him did not disturb him: he had become used to being stared at in England, and here the stares seemed not contemptuous, just curious. He walked round the square – the traffic was light – and then up the street which the barman had told him led to the station. Just before one of the buildings of the American University there was a side street, and out of this street, which Saman was about to cross, came Ronald. They nearly collided.

'Sorry,' said Saman, smiling.

'Not at all,' replied Ronald, giving the young Chinese-Thai an appreciative look, and returning the smile. Ronald was delighted to meet Saman, who revived happy memories of sojourns in Bangkok. 'You're from Thailand, aren't you?'

'Yes. How you know?'

'I've been to Thailand several times. I thought you looked Thai.'

'Thank you.'

'Where are you going?'

Saman showed Ronald a leaf of a Hilton Hotel message pad on which was written in Arabic and English, 'Bab-el-Louk'. 'I want go there.'

'Bab-el-Louk? Why?'

'I want go to Nile College.'

'Good Heavens!' exclaimed Ronald. 'I teach there. It's a bit late to go to the College now, and anyway it's Friday and it's been closed all day. Why do you want to go there?'

'I have friend there,' admitted Saman, his black eyes looking away from Ronald.

'Oh?'

'She English. She my teacher in England. Her name—'

'Joan Webber.' Ronald supplied the name first.

Saman turned his eyes back to Ronald's. 'You know her?'

'Nile College is not a big school. She's the only other English teacher. Anyway, let me show you Bab-el-Louk station. It's not far. My name is Ronald Wood, by the way.'

'My name Saman Panichakul. But call me Saman. Family name in Thailand too difficult.'

They began to walk towards the station. Ronald kept glancing at Saman, admiring his sleek black hair, his finely chiselled lips, his small India-rubber nose. How enticingly oriental he looked! They talked of Cairo, about the length of his stay, and Bangkok. 'Look,' Ronald said, 'I'm going to Nile College tomorrow morning. I could take you there in my car.'

'What time?'

'I leave here at eight in the morning. A bit early for you, perhaps, and Joan may have a class. I suggest you go to the College at noon, or later. I'll give her a message and she can ring you. You're at the Hilton, aren't you?'

'How you know?'

'That piece of paper you showed me had the name of the hotel on it.'

'I want to give her surprise. I mus' go to Nile College.'

'It might be an unpleasant surprise if you arrived there in the morning, and your arrival would cause a stir among the students, who would be curious.'

'What I do?'

'I suggest I bring her to the Hilton tomorrow. I'll not tell her you're here. Have you had dinner?'

'Pardon?'

'Have you eaten?'

'No.'

'Let us dine together.'

'Where? At my hotel?'

'No. I'll take you to a restaurant.'

'You're very kind.'

Ronald took Saman to the Estoril Restaurant, which was not far away. They dined on minestrone and spaghetti Napolitana – Saman had two helpings of the spaghetti, but unlike Ronald, he refused a chocolate ice cream. They talked of Bangkok. The young Thai told Ronald about his family. Apart from a married sister, he was the only child and had had a sheltered upbringing. He attended an expensive private school, to which he was taken in a chauffeured Daimler until he was old enough to drive himself to school. The family had five cars. Saman was forbidden to have a motor-scooter by his doting parents. They lived in a large modern house with an extensive garden, not far from the centre of Bangkok.

In 1937, at the age of twenty-five, Saman's father had emigrated with his parents from Shanghai to join a cousin who had a grocery store in the Chinese quarter of Bangkok. It was twelve years before the Communists led by Mao Tse-Tung defeated Chiang Kai-shek's army, but Shanghai was in turmoil owing to the civil war between the communists and the nationalists which was compounded by the Japanese invasion of China.

Saman's grandfather, Wong Fung-Moh took the Thai surname, Panichakul, but he did not long survive in his adoptive land. His son, Saman's father, married a Thai girl and gradually expanded the grocery business and by 1950 when Saman was five it had become a prosperous concern involving banking, insurance and property development.

It was the father who had insisted that his only son go to England when he was twenty to learn English properly. The British Council in Bangkok had recommended the language school in Hove. Saman was a comparatively innocent young man when he left to England in 1965. Still a mother's boy he had been initiated into sex by a fellow student who took him to a brothel. He had not enjoyed the automatic performances of prostitutes and had shunned the professional advances of bar hostesses. Joan had aroused in him a desire he had not known before. He fell madly in love with her.

Ronald listened to Saman's account of his background with attention. He had guessed because of his eyes that he had Chinese blood in his veins. He was surprised and flattered that the Thai had been so forthcoming to him a stranger. In order to test Saman's reaction Ronald mentioned a notorious gay bar in the Pat Pong district of Bangkok, but the Thai did not seem to have heard of it.

It was agreed that Ronald should bring Joan to the Hilton the following afternoon. He promised not to tell Joan the reason for taking her to the hotel. Saman was anxious to give her a surprise. Just before they parted Saman said, 'I forget your name. I'm sorry.'

Ronald told him and Saman took the wind out of his sails by saying, 'May I call you "uncle"?'

'If you like. You can call me "Uncle Ron".'

'Goodbye, Uncle Ron.'

☪

Ronald broke his promise not to tell Joan about Saman's arrival when they met in the morning interval.

'Oh God!' she said.

'Are you free this afternoon? I am. I could take you to the Hilton.'

'I'm supposed to meet Violet Brent at the Semiramis at six.'

'You could meet Saman at four or ring Violet and put her off.'

'Violet isn't put-offable.'

'Anyway you could see Saman at four. He's longing to see you. He can't wait.'

The bell rang for classes to recommence.

'OK,' said Joan. 'I shall have to meet him. The poor boy has come all the way from England to see me.'

'You're lucky to be so wanted.'

'Wish I weren't.' She hurried away, her arms loaded with exercise books.

Ronald telephoned Saman and told him he'd bring Joan to see him at four o'clock.

☪

On the previous evening Saman had not gone straight to bed when Ronald said *au revoir* to him in the lobby of the Hilton. Instead, he went for a stroll along the pavement by the great river. Being afraid of muggers, he did not venture far; he confined his promenade to a short patrol up and down opposite the hotel. Several young men importuned him, but he managed to brush them off. While leaning against the iron railing that prevented strollers from falling onto the embankment by the river, he spotted waddling towards him a short, portly, grey-haired European, whom he soon recognized. Oliver glanced at Saman, started to pass him, glanced again and stopped. 'Er, haven't we met before?' he asked diffidently. 'Aren't you . . .?'

'My name Saman. We meet in London with Joan Webber. You with wife. We have dinner at Caprice restaurant.'

'Of course, excuse me, I remember; this path is so badly lit.' Oliver held out a hand which Saman, smiling, took. 'What are you doing here?'

'I come to see Joan.'

'Oh? I'm here with Violet, my wife. We're at the Semiramis. Are you on your way to Thailand?'

'No. I go back England.'

'What a coincidence that we should meet! Where are you staying?'

'I stay at Hilton.' Saman waved a hand at the hotel.
'Oh? Is it good?'
'Hilton?'
'Yes.'
'I just come today. I meet English teacher. His name Lonald – I forget other name.'
'You must mean Ronald Wood.'
'Yes. He give me dinner.'
'Oh, he did, did he? May I give you a nightcap?'
'I no understand.'
'Would you like to have a drink with me?' asked Oliver, wondering if Saman, who looked sexy, was, as he had heard, like many Thais, bisexual; he would, Oliver thought, be more reliable than a riverside pick-up.
'No, thank you. I go to bed. I tired.'
'It's strange that you should meet two English people on the same evening; one who knows Joan, and me.'
'Yes, it strange.'
Oliver wondered why Joan, who had been Saman's teacher had not taught him the copulative verb; perhaps being in love she didn't like to correct his English. 'Well,' said Oliver, 'I'm sure we'll meet again. I'm Oliver Brent, in case you've forgotten, and I'm staying at the Semiramis, just past the bridge, near the British Embassy. So I'll say goodnight, Mister, Mister er—'
'Saman. Goodnight sir.'
The young Thai returned to the Hilton. Oliver continued his cruise and was soon accosted by a young Egyptian.

☪

'Where have you been?' Violet asked Oliver.
'A stroll.'
Oliver had hoped that his wife would have gone to bed when he returned to their suite in the Semiramis.
'You look as if you'd been running.'
'Do I?'

'And dishevelled. You haven't been up to some adventure, have you?'

'I met Saman.'

'Who?'

'Saman. Joan's ex-pupil or boyfriend or whatever.'

Violet bristled, took off her reading glasses and put her book on the occasional table in the sitting-room – joint territory, Oliver called it. 'You mean that young Thai?'

'Precisely.'

'What's he doing here?'

'Come to see Joan.'

'Oh, has he?'

'He must be very fond of her,' said Oliver. 'He's not on his way back to Thailand, as I at first thought. He came here especially to see her, apparently.'

'Damn him!'

'Darling, I'm dead tired. I simply must go to bed.'

'So you did have an adventure. Not with Saman, I suppose. You do look as if you'd been in a fight. Did Saman resist your advances?'

'Goodnight, Violet.'

Oliver went into his bedroom, undressed, had a shower and got into bed.

☪

Oliver's 'adventure' as Violet called it – he cursed her clairvoyant powers – had nearly been a disaster. The young Egyptian had taken him in a taxi to a dilapidated quarter on the other side of the river. They alighted at the head of an alley and after about fifty yards the young man drew from his pocket a large key and unlocked the rough, rickety door of a small one-storey dwelling. They entered a largish room furnished with two beds and little else; off the bedroom was another room, a kitchen or a bathroom which remained unlit. The boy left the key in the lock on the inside. Oliver proceeded to take off his jacket, his tie, his shirt, his shoes and his trousers and stood in his underwear and his socks before the boy, who pulled his sweater over his head and undid the buttons of his shirt. The electric bulb in the ceiling was of minimal voltage and Oliver could not see clearly the Egyptian's features. He was young, had long, straight, black hair and was slim; his chest seemed to be hairless.

'How much you give me?' asked the boy.

'Er, I don't know. How much do you want?'

'One hundred dollars.'

Oliver emitted a derisive laugh.' Too much.'

'OK,' said the Egyptian, threateningly. He went into the other room and came out with a knife. Whereupon Oliver, practised in undressing and dressing at speed, regained his shirt.

'OK,' said Oliver, pulling on his trousers. 'What about fifty?'

'Fifty no good. I want one hundred.' The youth brandished the knife.

'Well, we'll see,' said Oliver. 'I'll give you after.'

'I want now.'

Oliver seized his tweed jacket from the bed, trod into his loafers, hurled himself towards the door, pulled the key out of the lock, opened the door, turned out the light, threw the key across the room and ran into the alley; he kept running until he reached the main road where he waved wildly at a taxi, which mercifully was empty. His calculation that the young man would not leave his house without first finding the key and locking the door proved correct; glancing behind Oliver saw he was not being followed. Puffing, he leant back in the taxi and gave a sigh of relief. As the taxi was passing over the bridge, he put a hand to his neck and discovered that he had forgotten his tie. 'Well, the wretch got something out of me,' he said to himself. 'An expensive tie, one I bought at an airport and supposedly designed by a leading couturier.'

☪

'Remember, you've got to pretend that meeting Saman is a complete surprise,' Ronald said to Joan. 'You must put on an act of astonishment.'

They were in Ronald's car going along the right bank of the Nile towards the Hilton Hotel.

'I don't know how I'm going to do that convincingly as you've told me he is here.'

'Try your best, please,' pleaded Ronald, who had given his word to Saman that he would not tell Joan of his presence in Cairo and pretend to her that he was taking her to the Hilton to meet a friend of his.

Saman was waiting in the lobby and as soon as he saw Joan and Ronald enter the hotel, he hurried towards them.

'Saman!' cried Joan, simulating surprise unconvincingly. 'Fancy seeing you here! How wonderful to see you! When did you arrive?'

'Yesterday.'

'Are you on a tour?'

'Yes, but I come to see you.'

'How sweet!'

'I was going to Nile College, but Lonald who I met – did he tell you?'

'Yes. No,' she replied tentatively.

'He say better bring you here. I want surprise you.'

'You certainly have, Saman! It's marvellous to see you.'

'Thank you.'

They were still standing in the lobby, guests and their luggage moving past them. Ronald decided he should go. 'Well,' he said, 'I expect you have a lot to say to each other. I'll leave you to it.' He turned to Saman. 'It was good to meet you.'

Saman put his palms together in a Thai-style farewell and bowed his head slightly. 'See you,' Ronald said. 'Cheerio, Joan.'

He left the two lovers with a slight feeling of jealousy. No one had ever flown from England to see him.

☪

It was 6.30. Violet and Oliver were in their private sitting-room. Both with novels, which lay open on their laps.

'She should be here,' said Violet.

'He should be here too,' said her husband.

'As a teacher one would think she would be punctual.'

'I don't know whether Egyptian bankers are punctual or not.'

'They ought to be,' said Violet.

Oliver picked up his book.

'You're not still reading *Nicholas Nickleby*, are you?'

'You can see I am.'

'I don't know how you can read that childish stuff.'

'You know I read a Dickens novel every year,' said Oliver, defensively. 'I read *David Copperfield* last year.'

'Dickens' characters are so unreal,' remarked Violet, 'and so vulgar and inelegant.'

'They're caricatures, yet so human, and talking about reality, *The Count of Monte Cristo* is a fantasy.'

'I love it,' insisted Violet.

'I suppose you love it because of the hint of lesbianism in the story.'

'Dickens wouldn't have dared touch upon such a subject. French novels of the last century are much more adult than English ones. Nineteenth-century English ones are for children.' Violet picked up her paperback edition of Dumas's story, a translation.

'Thus spake Virginia,' said Oliver returning to Nicholas's adventures in Portsmouth with the theatrical troupe.

The telephone rang.

'Ah!' they both cried.

Oliver was first at the 'phone. It was Joan. 'It's Joan for you, Violet.'

☪

'What's the time, Saman?' Joan asked, drowsily. She, naked, was lying beside the young Thai, also naked, in his large bed. Both had fallen asleep after making love, an activity at which Saman excelled.

'I don't know,' he mumbled and turned on his left side, away from Joan.

Joan got up, crossed the room, and looking at her watch on the dressing-table saw that it was nearly twenty-to-seven. 'Oh my God!' she exclaimed.

'What's the matter?'

'I shall be late.'

'Why you late? You have class?' Saman turned on his back and sat up.

'No. I promised to meet someone. I must go.'

'You come back. We eat together.'

'I'm sorry. I can't.'

'What I do?' Saman asked, forlorn.

Joan felt guilty. He had come all the way from England to see her. 'I'll put her off.'

'*Her?*'

'An Englishwoman. A friend. She's visiting here.'

☪

'Mr Ron. I busy.'

'Oh?'

Ronald and Khalid were naked and in bed together. The bed in the Cairo hutch was a narrow, single one and Ronald was ready to unlink himself from his friend's embrace; the close proximity of Khalid was becoming too much of a good thing. They disentangled themselves. Khalid started to dress.

'Aren't you going to have a bath?' asked Ronald.

'I late.'

'What for?'

'I must go, Mister Ron.'
'You're going to meet Oliver Brent.'
'How you know?'
'I guess. Am I right?'
'Yes.'
'Give him my love.'


☪


'Can't you come a little later, Joan?' said Violet into the phone . . .' How about tomorrow then? We must discuss the trip to Luxor . . . oh, all right.' She put down the phone.

'Not coming?'

'No.'

'I'm sorry.'

The two resumed their seats and not exchanging another word took up their books.

There came a knock upon the door.

'That would be your friend, I suppose.' Violet rose. 'I'll leave you to it.'

'Don't go. I'd like you to meet him.'

'No, thanks.' She went into her bedroom.

The knock was repeated.

Oliver opened the door to Khalid. The Egyptian entered quickly and looked around the room as if he were expecting to see someone else.

'She's not here,' said Oliver.

'Who, Mister Olli?'

'The woman who was here last time. Have a drink?' Oliver was at the sideboard about to pour out a whisky.

'No thanks.'

'You sure?'

Oliver led Khalid into his bedroom.

☪

Tahrir Square began to fill with a motley crowd of Cairenes: many in jellabas, some with turbans, others with small skull caps, some in suits, others in slacks and pullovers, some women in black abbayas, others in dresses with coats. Dusk was gathering. All were excited. Nasser was going to speak from the balcony of the *mougamma* (government) building, a huge modern block that took up nearly the whole southern side of the vast square, the hub of Cairo; in the middle was an empty plinth on which a planned statue of the Khedive Ismael had never been placed; there was much controversy about whose image should be put there.

Saman – ignorant of Egypt and the problems of the Middle East – joined the crowd in the square outside the Hilton. Oliver and Violet had walked to the Hilton from the Semiramis nearby. Oliver had thought it prudent to stand near the Hilton so that if there were any anti-Western demonstrations they could escape into the hotel.

'Look, there's Saman,' said Oliver to his wife.

'Who?'

'Saman, the Thai, Joan's friend. I told you he was here. I'll call him over.' Oliver squeezed through the crowd and brought Saman back to where his tall and sturdy wife was standing. Violet greeted the young Thai with distant politeness. 'How long are you staying?' she asked.

Saman's quiet answer was drowned by the boisterous cheers of the crowd. When Nasser came forward on the balcony of the *mougamma* building, the tightly packed gathering fell silent. The president held his audience like a great actor, altering the volume of his sonorous voice. He began with the word Islam (peace), stressing the meaning of the word with its grammatical variations. Even the Brents and Saman, who couldn't understand a word, were moved. Nasser did not speak in classical Arabic, which was customary for public speeches, but in the demotic parlance of the people and this endeared him to them. When the speech and the cheering were over, the crowd dispersed calmly. The posses of armed police posted throughout the square were not required to quell any unruly outburst.

'I want to know what he said,' Violet demanded,

'The speech will be in the *Mail* tomorrow,' Oliver informed his wife. 'Let's have a drink.'

They went into the hotel.

Saman, uncertain as to whether he was invited, hesitated in the lobby.

'Aren't you going to join us, Saman?' asked Oliver.

They sat in the bar. Oliver ordered drinks.

'What did you think of Nasser's speech?' Violet asked Saman.

'I no understand.'

'Nor did I, but didn't you think it sounded marvellous? Fine oratory.'

'Maybe.'

'Joan Webber and I,' said Violet, pointedly, emphasising the name,' are thinking of going to Luxor.'

'Why don't we all go together?' suggested Oliver.

'I thought you had other plans,' said Violet sharply.

'They were only ideas,' replied her husband. 'Nothing fixed.'

'How we go?' asked Saman.

'In our car,' said Oliver. 'If you came we'd have three drivers, four if Joan can drive. Can she?'

'I've no idea,' said Saman.

'No, she can't,' said Violet, showing that she knew Joan better than Saman did. She kicked Oliver under the table.

The Brents rose to go. 'Excuse us, Saman,' said Violet. 'We have a dinner engagement.'

When they had gone, Saman signed the bill, which Oliver hadn't paid, and went into the coffee shop to dine alone. He pondered the suggestion of their going to Luxor and of Violet's and Oliver's relationship with Joan.

☪

'What am I to do?' asked Joan.

'It's hard for me to advise,' Ronald answered. 'I don't know what you want.'

'Nor do I.' Joan was tearful.

They were in their apartment building at Nile College. Lessons were over. They had lunched in the school dining-hall after the younger students had eaten. Ramadan had begun and the older students fasted and were proud to do so as it meant they had reached manhood; there were no afternoon classes during the holy month. Joan had invited Ronald to have some cake in her flat and he had found it difficult to refuse. He was beginning to like her or at least to find her more than tolerable, in any case she spoke the same language, which was a relief after the students' mauled English and his having to enunciate sentences slowly and distinctly.

'I'm not happy here,' announced Joan, after a pause and a munching of a piece of cake. 'Are you?'

'Up to a point, yes. I like being in Egypt and I find the Egyptians pleasant people to be with.'

'They hate us,' complained Joan. 'At the assembly this morning that mealy-mouthed English teacher, Mr Thomas, was again crowing about the killing of another British soldier in Aden.'

'They don't hate us,' Ronald contradicted. 'They hate our government's policy. They think that Britain still wants to control them. We've been through all this before. They don't hate us, by us I mean you and me. They're patriotic, not xenophobic; most of them may be illiterate, but they are very civilized.'

'They pour out anti-British propaganda.'

'One can't blame them if they do. You must forgive me if I'm repeating myself but what I have to say bears repetition. You must realize that this is the first time that Egypt has been truly independent for centuries. They were ruled by the Mamelukes, then by the Ottomans, by us – Cromer. And when they were granted independence in the thirties, they weren't truly in control of their own affairs. The British army were in Abbassia Barracks in Cairo and in the Canal bases. In the war our army was in Egypt and in control. When in 1942 Rommel was almost at the gates of Alexandria and there were rumours of a pro-Axis movement favoured by King Farouk, the British ambassador, Sir Miles Lampson, had Abdin Palace surrounded by British troops and forced a change of government. And now they are independent. Nasser has given them hope. No longer do they feel despised "wogs".'

'Despised what?' asked Joan.

'Wogs, a pejorative for Egyptians, or considered as a pejorative for some reason. It means "worthy oriental gentleman".'

'What's wrong with that?'

'It's taken to be sarcastic, I suppose. Now, King Farouk—'

'Oh please, Ronald. That's enough of your Egyptian lecture for today. Let's get back to my problem.'

'What *is* your problem?' asked Ronald, who had a pretty good idea of what it was.'

'I've told you a bit about it before, but not in detail—'

Ronald moved forward in his uncomfortable armchair, whose back if leant against reclined, thus making the sitter almost horizontal. 'I'm the height of discretion, you know. You can confide in me with confidence.'

'Well,' Joan recommenced. 'Saman, whom you've met, was a student at the language school I taught at in Hove—'

'I know that much,' Ronald said.

Joan frowned. 'I'll go on. If I repeat myself, please don't interrupt. Saman and I had an affair, which I tried to get out of; not that I didn't find him exciting. I did. I loved his being oriental, being different and he seemed to be so rich and had such good manners. I come from a lower middle-class family who while not exactly poor could never splurge. To be with someone who found it quite ordinary to buy luxuries, to eat expensively was to me wonderful. I didn't love him for his money, his free spending—'

'No, of course not,' Ronald put in.

'Please, Ronald. Do you want me to go on?'

'Yes, please. Do.'

'And then at the theatre in London Saman and I sat next Violet and Oliver Brent, and after the show they insisted on us dining with them at the Caprice, which to me was a great thrill. Saman was bored with them. I could see, though, that Oliver liked him—'

'He would.'

'I didn't realize her motive at that first meeting, and I was surprised when she asked for my address and wrote it down in her diary when we were in the loo together.'

'Did she make a pass, or whatever women do in the loo?' Ronald asked.

'No. We were not alone. But she sent me an invitation for the weekend on a picture postcard – the picture was a photo of the Brents' huge mansion. I was intrigued. To satisfy my curiosity about Violet and the house at Tring, I accepted.'

Joan paused and took another piece of cake, which Ronald eyed covetously.

'And you were seduced by Violet,' Ronald added.

Joan nodded while masticating. She swallowed and said, 'I mentioned that to you before.'

'Yes, I remember when we were going into Cairo on the way to meet Violet and Oliver. Never mind, tell me again.'

'I don't know why I succumbed to her entreaties,' Joan continued. 'She's very persuasive and at the same time grand, and the environment, the great house, the luxury were beguiling.'

'Did you enjoy it?'

'Yes, I must admit I did.'

'More than with Saman?'

'No, not more than with Saman. It was different, more sensual somehow.'

'So they're both after you?'

'Yes.'

'And you're bisexual?'

'No. I don't think so. Apart from a few pashes at school, I'd never thought about being a lesbian.'

'Lesbians are often bisexual,' muttered Ronald, sententiously, more to himself than to Joan.

'The point of all this is what am I going to do?'

Ronald was silent for a moment. He then said portentously, 'You must do what you think wise.'

'I wouldn't have started on all this if I thought you'd only come up with useless advice. "Do what you think wise,"' Joan repeated, angrily and bitterly, 'What on earth is the use of saying that?'

Ronald, taken aback by Joan's virulence, said, weakly, 'Sorry.' For the first time Ronald scrutinised Joan carefully; before, he hadn't bothered to assimilate her looks. She was well-covered and had a full bosom; such embonpoint Arabs found irresistible; Ronald remembered a Thai in Chiang Mai who had told him he dreamed of big Western women with ample breasts – perhaps this was what Saman liked, although Joan was small of stature. Ronald, unobservant about women, had realized she was attractive: blonde with blue-grey eyes (he had noticed that); now he took in her features and was struck by her straight elegant nose and her sensual lips and a slightly prominent chin; the last suggested determination, yet she had submitted to Violet's inducements.

'Well,' said Joan, 'What do you suggest?'

'What are your own feelings? Are you in love with Saman or Violet? Where lies your heart?'

Joan laughed. 'Where lies my heart? What a question! I don't know, to tell you the truth, that it lies anywhere.'

Ronald leant back in his armchair. 'Obviously you can't marry Saman,' he began.

'Why not?'

'Oh, if you think you could, go ahead. Has he proposed to you?'

'No.'

'He must be very fond of you to make a special trip to Egypt to see you.'

'He is. I'm sure.'

'Well,' said Ronald, looking at the ceiling as he was almost flat in his chair. 'Tell him you'll marry him after a year or so; tell him you need time to think it over, which is reasonable; after all you'd have to live in Thailand and that would mean a completely different life for you. As regards Violet, you can't marry her, so tell her you're going to marry Saman. That will put an end to her importunities.'

'Oh no it won't. She's not one to give up. And—' Joan paused.

'And what?' asked Ronald impatiently.

'I like her and I have given in to her.'

'Well then, there's no more to say. I've now advised you.' Ronald struggled forward to a sitting position. 'What an awful chair this is! One is either perched or prostrate.'

'It's not mine. It belongs to the College.'

'Yes, yes. I wasn't blaming you for it. By the way, I have a problem too.'

'Don't tell me about it, if you don't want to,' Joan said.

'It's simply this,' Ronald went on, noticing that while he'd been lying back in the chair the cake had been consumed. 'Oliver Brent is having an affair with my Egyptian friend, Khalid. And being rich or having a rich wife, Oliver gives him more money than I can afford to.'

'If it's a matter of money and not affection,' said Joan, 'I should give him up.'

'I love him.'

'You'll get over it.' Joan no longer the supplicant had become the counsellor. 'At your age—'

'Age doesn't come into it,' Ronald said, indignantly.

'At your age,' Joan repeated firmly, 'you must be sensible. If he loves you more than Oliver's money, he'll come back to you—'

'He hasn't left me yet, but there's a danger that—'

'So make a break. Teach him a lesson.'

'It's difficult. He's just what I like. He suits me.' Ronald surprised himself by making this confession to this young woman. He rose. 'We haven't solved our problems, I'm afraid. Things will work out, perhaps.'

'Let's hope so,' Joan said meekly, no longer the practical counsellor.

☪

While tourists and temporary residents like Joan and Ronald did not take much interest in the situation that smouldered on the frontiers between Israel and her Arab neighbours, the danger of the smouldering bursting into flames became more real, and the campaign in the Aden Protectorate continued in a desultory manner with occasional flare-ups. The average Cairene continued his daily struggle; he lived from day to day not thinking about war or the possibility of war; he was aware though of the tension on the Sinai border (the antagonists were kept apart by United Nations observers), but Sinai was wide and seemed far away.

Some opposed the government. Among university students there were subversive elements, but opposition was kept under control by the secret police. It was not a free society, but with a huge population steadily increasing, such a society would have been difficult to cope with. The ousting of King Farouk in 1952, the nationalization of the Suez Canal (the British claim that the Egyptian pilots were not capable of running the vital waterway had proved wrong) had been popular, so had the expropriation of the large agricultural estates. The pashas no longer had any power, the main source of their wealth had gone.

☪

Violet and Oliver belied Cedric's condemnation of their idleness. Violet was making a serious survey of the Mamcluke mosques and Oliver spent the mornings in the Cairo museum studying the artifacts of ancient Egypt. He had the idea of writing a guide to those exhibits which were displayed in the darker rooms and were often missed by tourists, also in the darker rooms a guardian in a dark-blue uniform would sometimes appear and for a few minutes Oliver's studies would be interupted. He and his wife would set out on their different projects around 10 in the morning and meet at Groppi's for lunch at 1.30; there they might see Cedric or Ronald and Saman might join them.

Ramadan, of which the foreigners had taken no notice apart from remarking that in the evenings the streets seemed more crowded than usual with merrymakers who had just broken their fast, culminated with the Id el Fitr and this year it more or less coincided with Christmas. It was holiday time for Westerners and Muslims, the Copts celebrated their Christmas twelve days later as they followed the Orthodox calendar. One lunchtime Violet and Oliver went up to the table in Groppi's at which Ronald and Cedric were sitting.

'May we join you?' asked Oliver with his hand on the back of a chair.

Cedric grunted. Ronald rose, flapping his napkin 'Of course,' he said. 'Good to see you.'

Violet sat next to Ronald on the banquette seat; Oliver sat by Cedric, who had begun his omelette.

'I've been at Ibn Tulun all morning,' said Violet.

'The greatest mosque in Cairo,' mumbled Cedric, while chewing a piece of ham omelette. He swallowed and added, 'built in the best period.'

'We're going to Luxor for Christmas,' said Violet.

'I hope you've booked,' said Cedric. 'The place is likely to be full at this time of the year.'

Violet looked at Oliver. 'You'd better book, dear.'

'But we don't know what day we're arriving.' Oliver turned to Cedric. 'We're going by the Red Sea coast.'

'Oh yes,' he replied, uninterested.

'What are you going to do over the holidays?' asked Oliver of no one in particular.

'I shall be working,' said Cedric, smugly.

'I've no plans,' said Ronald, though he hoped to take Khalid somewhere in his car.

☪

The party to Luxor did not seem to be turning out as some of the travellers had hoped it would. After Oliver had expressed his disapproval of his wife's plan to go to Luxor alone with Joan in the Jaguar, he had insisted on accompanying them. Violet had been agreeable to this; he would be complaisant. But she made it clear that she would not countenance Saman joining the party as Oliver had suggested over the drinks in the bar of the Hilton after Nasser's speech. The 'dinner engagement' had been invented by Violet so that no further arrangements about the trip could be discussed. The kick under the table was a signal she had often used to shift her husband.

'Why must that Thai come with us?' Violet asked Joan angrily. They were in Violet's bedroom at the Semiramis and were near to having a row about Saman.

Joan did not yield. 'If he doesn't come with us, I'll not go. He made the journey to Cairo expressly to see me,' Joan reminded Violet, not for the first time.

'And he smokes,' complained Violet, vehemently.

'Not all the time.'

'I cannot allow smoking in my car.'

'I'll ask him not to smoke in the car.'

'You're in love with him, aren't you?' Violet challenged; still vehement.

'I don't know.'

'You don't know?' Violet's fury was formidable. Joan was determined to stand up to her. 'What about me?' demanded Violet in a melodramatic tone, pointing to her chest.

'I'm very fond of you, Violet,' Joan replied softly.

'But you love that Thai.'

'I said I didn't know if I loved him.'

'We'd better cancel the trip.'

'All right, if you feel like that, let's cancel it.'

Violet stormed out of the bedroom and finding the sitting-room empty, she banged on Oliver's door. 'Oliver! Oliver!'

Oliver was in bed with Khalid. After emitting an 'Oh Lord!', he cried, irritably, 'What is it?'

'I want to speak to you.'

'Not now, Violet. Later.'

'I wish to speak to you *now*.'

'Oh Lord!' Oliver exclaimed again, getting out of bed and going to the door. 'What is it, Violet?'

Violet rattled the door-handle. 'Come out,' she commanded.

And, as usual, Oliver obeyed. 'Wait a moment,' he said. He put on his dressing-gown, and giving Khalid's erect prick a squeeze, whispered, 'Just stay as you are. Won't be a moment.' He unlocked the door and entered the sitting-room, closing the door quickly. 'What is it, dear?' he asked his wife, who stood fuming.

'Joan wants Saman to come with us to Luxor,' she snarled.

'That'll let me out,' returned Oliver, ignoring Violet's fury. 'I don't want to go and Saman can help you with the driving.'

'Oh don't you *see*,' she said, her anger unabated.

Joan came out of Violet's bedroom, and Khalid, dressed, appeared from Oliver's room at the same time.

'I must go, I'm afraid,' Joan said with unaccustomed firmness.

Oliver turned to Khalid. 'Don't tell me you're going too.'

'Yes.' Khalid stood for a moment appraising Joan.

After hesitating, Oliver adjusted the cord of his dressing-gown and addressed the young Egyptian. 'This is my wife, and this is Joan Webber.' Khalid shook the hands of the two women who received his polite greeting with surprise, raising their eyebrows and smiling weakly. Khalid left the room followed by Joan.

'Now see what you've done!' Oliver glared at Violet, strode back into his bedroom and slammed the door.

☪

Ronald was relieved when the holy month of Ramadan was over as Khalid would abstain from sex until dusk when the gun went off signalling the end of the daytime fast. Khalid would undress and lie naked alongside Ronald in the inadequate bed, but no lovemaking was allowed until the gun had fired. When the boom sounded, followed by cheers from the people in the street below who were aching to break their fast, Khalid would permit lust to begin. Ronald wondered why his friend didn't want to eat first. Perhaps Khalid like many Cairenes only pretended to fast and had secret snacks during the day. Did his mother get up two hours before dawn to cook the early morning meal, which must be eaten before sunrise? Or did his wife or sister prepare the food for the family? Ronald knew little about his friend's family background and he regretted this. The Muslim purdah rule created a barrier and prevented social intercourse, particularly when a foreigner was concerned. Ronald did not like to pry and his Arabic wasn't good enough to hold an intelligent conversation with Khalid; the young man never mentioned his family. Ronald would have liked Khalid to be a companion and not just a sex friend, but this did not seem to be possible.

He was pleased when Khalid suggested that during the Muslim feast he take him to Suez and he readily agreed. They planned to spend the night in the famous port. Ronald was delighted that his friend had not arranged to go off somewhere with Oliver. He did not know that Oliver had unwillingly obeyed Violet's command that he go on the Luxor trip with her, Joan and Saman. The last, who had detached himself from his tourist group, did not require any persuading.

☪

From his bedroom Oliver entered the sitting-room of the suite, bearing a briefcase and a raincoat. He was wearing a charcoal grey, medium weight suit, a white shirt and a green tie. Violet was in an armchair reading the *Egyptian Mail*. She flicked her eyes up at her husband.

'You look as if you have a business appointment, not as if you're about to embark on a safari.'

Oliver defended his appearance by saying, 'I think it unwise of you to wear trousers. The Egyptians admire modesty in women, not their copying men's garb.'

'My dear,' returned Violet, 'I should say that the jellaba which most Egyptian males wear is more like a skirt than trousers. So my trousers are not going to upset anyone.'

Oliver, ignoring his wife's riposte, said quietly, 'I wish you'd change into a sensible skirt.'

'I'm not going to. I think you ought to change into a sensible outfit. You look ridiculous in that suit.'

The telephone rang.

'That will be Joan,' said Violet. 'Have you packed?'

'Yes.'

'You've not forgotten your dinner-jacket, have you?' Violet picked up the phone. 'Good,' she said. 'Is Saman with you? . . . he would be . . . nothing. We'll be down instantly.'

☪

There was a knock on the shaky door of Ronald's Cairo abode. Ronald had been sitting on what his Armenian landlord called the terrace and he referred to as the garden; it contained one pot plant, a hibiscus that had never bloomed. He rose and let in Khalid, who was wearing jeans and a sweater over an open neck shirt.

'You have no bag?' Ronald asked.

'Bag?'

'We're staying the night in Suez, aren't we?'

'I do not need.'

'Shall we go then? I've packed a few things.' He indicated a grip that was bulging. Khalid took it. 'It heavy, Mister Ron. What have you inside?'

'Things. Things for the night.' Ronald wished he were like Khalid and could travel with no luggage at all, but he was unable to spend a night without his pyjamas, his washing things, a bottle of after shave, a change of underwear, a clean shirt, socks, slippers, a dressing-gown and his medical supplies: aspirins, indigestion pills, Dettol ointment, Elastoplast, a tube of Preparation H, another of Nivea Cream, a packet of tissues, soap and a flywhisk.

They summoned the glass-sided lift and descended into the street.

'I must get some petrol,' said Ronald, glancing at the gauge; he had forestalled Khalid's attempt to get into the driving seat.

In retaliation Khalid turned on the radio, which he knew Ronald didn't like. Above the wail of a female Arab voice, Khalid said, 'Mister Ron you have camera?'

'No.'

'Without camera, journey no good.'

'My camera is in my flat at the school.'

'We go get.'

☪

Saman was at the wheel of the Jaguar. Violet, at his side, a map open on her lap, was worrying about the speed at which he was driving. Oliver sat in the back with Joan. He would have preferred Saman to be in her place. He had offered to take over the driving from Violet but she had asked Saman to do so; Oliver felt that this was a way of snubbing him after his criticism of her wearing trousers. Joan too was in trousers. 'You're sensibly dressed,' Violet had said pointedly when they met in the hall of the Semiramis.

Suddenly the engine had a coughing fit.

'I told you not to drive so fast on this rough road,' Violet said.

The car jerked along for a while and then the engine cut out; after a hundred yards or so it came to a halt.

'What's the matter?' Oliver asked.

'I think the bumps have disconnected something,' Violet said. 'What do you think, Saman?'

'I not know,' the young man replied. There was just a faint buzz when he turned the ignition key, which he did several times.

'You'll run down the battery if you go on doing that,' Violet said, crossly.

'Perhaps we've run out of petrol,' Oliver suggested.

'The tank is over half full,' Violet said.

'How far are we from Suez?' Oliver asked.

'About ten miles I'd say,' Violet answered, looking at her map safari style.

Saman got out of the car, lit a cigarette and then opened the bonnet and gazed at the engine. Violet joined him, frowned at the cigarette and waved a hand. Oliver remained in the back with Joan.

'Oliver, you might help,' Violet shouted.

'I can't do anything,' Oliver told Joan. 'I know nothing about car engines.'

'Oliver!'

'Oh dear!' Oliver joined his wife and Saman and with them stared at the idle engine.

'Saman says it's the carburettor,' Violet informed her husband. 'He thinks dirt may have got into it.'

'The wretched thing only had a service the day before yesterday,' Oliver remarked.

'They probably only washed it,' Violet said. 'What are we going to do? We can't spend the night here.'

'We'll have to ask someone to tow us into Suez,' Oliver said.

'I don't like being towed.'

'We have no choice, duckie.' Oliver only dared used this doubtful endearment when he felt a bit superior.

☪

Khalid in his brief underpants stood on the diving board of the pool in the Grand Hotel at Suez, where he and Ronald had taken a room for the night. Ronald in bathing trunks was kneeling at the edge of the pool pointing his camera at his friend.

'Now,' Ronald directed, 'put your left hand on your hip, stretch out your right arm, hold your chest out, tummy in and smile.' Khalid liked having his photo taken and carried out the instructions to a T. 'Fine, Hold it.' Ronald pressed the exposure button. 'Now. Once more.'

Behind there were voices he recognized. He looked round and saw Violet, Oliver, Saman and Joan.

'Heavens!' he exclaimed. 'I thought you were going to Luxor.'

'The car broke down,' Oliver explained. 'We had to be towed to a garage.'

'We'll have to spend the night here,' Violet said with distaste.

Oliver was looking at Khalid on the diving board; the young Egyptian had relaxed his pose.

Oliver hailed him with a weak 'Hallo'. Khalid dived into the water and swam a fast and impressive crawl to the shallow end.

'Are you on your way to Luxor?' Oliver asked of Ronald.

'No. Just spending the night. Going back to Cairo tomorrow.'

'Oliver,' Violet commanded, 'we must see about rooms.'

At the reception desk a languid clerk in a black jacket looked vaguely at the passports of the four travellers and then from pigeon holes behind him took two keys. He handed one key to Oliver and the other to Saman, assuming he was with Joan. Violet sulked; she would have liked to switch keys with Saman.

'How funny that Ronald and Khalid are here,' Oliver remarked to Violet.

'Are you jealous?' his wife asked.

'No,' Oliver lied, of course not. 'Are you?'

'Don't be absurd.'

They went up to their rooms that overlooked the pool. During the ascent the cross-eyed lift boy in tarboosh and shabby jacket with gold-braided epaulettes and baggy Turkish-style trousers gave Oliver a mischievous look.

From their separate rooms the four went on to their balconies and looked at Ronald and Khalid splashing each other. Ronald pretended not to notice them and swam up the pool with Khalid. Oliver glanced at the adjacent balcony where Joan and Saman stood and said to Violet, 'This is rather like *Private Lives*.'

In spite of her ill humour, Violet laughed. 'A bigger cast, less manageable.'

☪

The six dined together. Violet assumed the role of hostess and dictated the *placement*: 'Now Joan, come on my right, Khalid – it is Khalid, isn't it? – on my left, then next to Joan, Ronald, and opposite Ronald, Saman. Oliver, you at the other end of the table.'

They took their seats. *Suffragis* brought white wine, which Oliver had already ordered, Clos Mariut, and began to pour it out. Khalid declined the wine and asked for beer. A crab dish appeared. Khalid hesitated accepting it until Ronald, not really knowing, said, 'Not *haram*.' The stuffed crab was followed by fillets of a Red Sea fish, which were excellent; the meal ended with crème caramel. The conversation was not fluent and not general. Violet talked to Joan in an undertone, Ronald to Oliver about the car, and Saman to no one. Khalid stared lasciviously at Joan.

Violet said quietly to Joan, 'I'm sorry about all this.'

'All what?' Joan replied quite loudly.

'The breakdown, this hotel, our having to stay in this awful town.'

'I find it fascinating.'

'There's nothing here, as far as I could see, except squalor.'

'I thought the place was full of atmosphere, Violet.'

'Well then, it's lucky we had to stop here.'

Oliver said to Ronald, 'D'you think the car will be ready in the morning?'

'I've no idea. The Egyptians are clever at improvising. My car needed some spare part recently and the garage fashioned a replacement out of bits and pieces from old cars. It worked perfectly.'

'I don't like the idea of a spare part made out of old bits and pieces.'

'The one they made for me seems to be fine,' returned Ronald.

In *sotto voce* Violet said to Joan, 'Come to my room after dinner.'

'I can't,' Joan whispered. 'There's Saman.'

Violet frowned. 'Bother him.' Turning to Khalid she said in her hostess's voice, 'Do you know Suez well?'

'This first time.'

'First time for me too. I never came here when I was in Cairo before.'

Ronald said to Saman, 'Are you enjoying your stay in Egypt?'

'It is interesting,' the Thai replied.

'In what way do you find it interesting?' Ronald asked.

Before answering, Saman glanced at Joan. 'It is different.'

'Different from Bangkok? Indeed it is. Very different.'

'Oh yes.' Saman looked down and attended to his fish.

Oliver said to Ronald, 'What'll we do if the car isn't ready tomorrow?'

'You have little choice. You must stay here until it is ready or have it towed back to Cairo.'

'They said at the garage that it would be ready by 10 in the morning.'

'Let's hope it will be. I wouldn't count on it though.'

After the crème caramel, which they all ate except for Khalid, who lit a cigarette, Violet said, 'Coffee? That is Egyptian or Turkish coffee, I suppose.'

'Well that is coffee, isn't it?' Oliver said. '*I* like it very much.'

Coffee was ordered and served. Saman took no more than one sip, but the others soon emptied their little cups. They rose from the table, and then followed a pause and a hesitation.

'Bed for me,' Ronald said, looking at Khalid.

'I'm going to take a walk,' Oliver announced.

'Joan,' Violet coaxed, 'I'd like to have a word with you.'

'Yes?' Joan, said returning from the dining-room threshold across which the others had passed.

'Come up to my room,' Violet ordered. 'I'll go up now. Join me there. Oliver is going for a walk. Get Saman to join him.'

'I'll see,' Joan replied doubtfully. She wasn't in the mood for Violet's overpowering passion and when the older woman had ascended to her bedroom, she joined Saman and Oliver in the hall and they went for a walk together in the dark and empty street.

Khalid watched Joan leave with the others and then a little unwillingly accompanied Ronald to their room.

'What time we go back tomorrow?' Khalid asked.

'In the morning. Not too early.'

After the two were in their separate beds, Khalid said, 'Miss Joan very beautiful.'

'D'you think so?' Ronald asked in a disparaging tone.

'Why she like that little Chinese man?'

'I don't know, Khalid. He's Thai, not Chinese.'

'He look Chinese.'

'Violet likes Joan very much. She's jealous of Saman.'

'*Ya salaam!*' exclaimed the Egyptian.

☪

Violet asked Oliver when he joined her in their bedroom after his walk where he had gone.

'Just down the street. The whole place seemed shut. There were some pimps about and some foreign merchant-seamen.'

'Why were you so long?' Violet was in bed with a book.

'We had a drink when we came back.'

'And Joan?'

'She went up to bed while Saman and I were finishing our brandies. I'd forget her if I were you. She obviously adores Saman.'

☪

'Lonald and that Egyptian man back to Cairo tomollow, light?'

'Yes,' Joan said.

They were in their separate beds.

'We go with them, OK?'

'Back to Cairo? What about Luxor? We're supposed to be going to Luxor with Violet and Oliver.'

'I know. But now I no want. Lonald's car got four seat. We can be at back, OK?'

Saman left his bed and got into Joan's.

'OK?' he repeated.

'OK,' she replied.

☪

Soon after 10 the next morning, Ronald and Khalid descended to the hall to find the others gathered. Oliver was in a state about the Jaguar. 'And when I got to the garage, the car was there, but half the engine was strewn along the pavement. They are sending to Cairo for a spare part.'

'How long will that take?' Violet asked anxiously.

'They said the car would be ready tomorrow.'

'Tomorrow?'

'Yes.'

Violet turned to Joan and Saman, whose bags the lift-boy had just brought down. 'You can tell him to take those up again. We'll have to spend another night here.'

Joan took a deep breath and confronted Violet, 'Saman said he must go back to Cairo. I think I ought to go with him. Ronald will take us in his car.'

'But we're going to Luxor as soon as our car is ready.'

'Saman doesn't want to go now. He says he'd better get back to Cairo. Officially he's on a package tour.'

'I see,' Violet said, much disconcerted. 'Well, goodbye, then,' she added curtly.

Goodbyes were said by all and Ronald, Khalid, Joan and Saman set off for Cairo in Ronald's little Fiat.

Violet and Oliver stood alone in the hall.

'Well!' Oliver exclaimed.

☪

During the previous night Violet had complained of Oliver's snoring; they had never shared a bedroom before. That night Oliver, having moved to another room, was visited by the cross-eyed lift-boy, who never seemed to be off duty. On being let into the room, the boy tore off his old-fashioned, Turkish-style uniform and slipping off his long cotton underpants threw himself upon Oliver.

The next day the car was still not ready, the spare part not having come from Cairo. And the following day it wasn't ready either. The Brents had to spend a week in Suez. Oliver was bored. After his visit to the garage in the morning, he had nothing to do except wait for the evening and the lift-boy's lightning visits. Almost next to the hotel was a Coptic church in which Violet took an interest. She met the bearded priests in charge and spent hours talking with one of them, who spoke passable English. When eventually the Jaguar was repaired and the Brents left Suez and returned to Cairo (the visit to Luxor was abandoned) the church and the lift-boy both received generous donations.

☪

By the time Violet and Oliver had returned to Cairo, Saman had left, school had begun and Joan and Ronald were back at work.

Violet's introduction to the Coptic Church had aroused her interest. She gave up her study of early Islamic architecture and took up the Copts. Every mornong she went to the Coptic Museum and the Coptic cathedral and made friends with a venerable priest whose face was mostly obscured by his copious beard; his eyes were bright and pierced his interlocutor's like an occulist's examining torch. Violet told Oliver that he was intelligent.

Meanwhile Oliver wasn't progressing either with his desultory study of the minor artifacts of ancient Egypt or with his novel, which he had vaguely begun at Tring. As at home he only managed a few sentences a day. The trouble was that he hadn't decided on a theme for his book. 'Just write away,' he had been told, 'and ideas will come.' He had also heard people say, 'You must decide on how the story will end before you begin.' So he tried to write his novel backwards, but this didn't work. However the mornings crept by and he would meet Violet, hot from her Coptic researches in Groppi's for lunch.

Soon after Violet and Oliver had sat down at a table one lunchtime, Cedric appeared and asked if he could join them.

'What do you know about the Copts?' Violet asked him before he was seated.

'The Copts?'

'Yes, the Copts,' she said fiercely.

'They're a Christian minority. They date back before Islam, of course. They like to think of themselves as descendants of the ancient Egyptians, those who resisted conversion to Islam. They're mostly found in Assuyt in upper Egypt. There's a community in Fayoum and monasteries in Wadi Natrun, between Cairo and Alexandria.'

Violet turned to Oliver. 'We must go there.'

'Where, darling?'

'To Fayoum and Assuyt.'

'I had thought,' said Oliver, 'of going to Fayoum before. But not to see the Copts. It's an oasis, isn't it?'

'Yes, sort of, and there's a lake, with fish, sort of trout.' Cedric, not interested in the Copts or knowledgeable about them changed the subject. 'By the way,' he said, 'the situation looks dangerous.'

'What situation?' asked Violet.

'Is it a meatless day?' asked Oliver of the waiter, who nodded. 'Though Curzon said no gentleman has soup for luncheon, I'll have the lentil soup – I adore lentil soup – and chicken livers with rice. What'll you have, Violet?'

'I'll have the same,' she replied abstractedly. 'Tell me about the situation, Cedric.'

'Tension is building up on the frontier between Egypt and Israel,' Cedric explained.

'What are you going to have, Cedric,?' asked Oliver.

'A tomato omelette and a demi-carafe of red wine.'

'What about the war in the Yemen?' asked Violet.

'It goes on,' Cedric answered.

'Who's winning?'

'No one. The British in Aden are on the defensive.'

'That's not unusual,' Oliver said. 'Ought we, by we I mean Violet and I, to leave?'

'No, I don't think so, not yet anyway. There's a United Nations force stationed between the two sides.'

'Armed with blue berets, I suppose,' Oliver stated.

☪

The pupils at Nile College were very much aware of the situation and were wholly behind Nasser. Since the meeting at Suez and the drive to Cairo with Joan and Saman, the two English teachers had begun to see more of each other at the College. It was the possibility of war and the fact that they came from the same country that brought them together. Ronald decided that Joan, as a person, was acceptable, and as a platonic friend, possible. Now and then they exchanged confidences. One afternoon over tea, which Joan liked to have when classes were over, she told Ronald that she had had enough of Violet.

'She's so overwhelming. She wants to eat one up.'

'Possessive?' Ronald suggested.

'That's hardly the word. She's like an octopus with all tentacles grabbing at me. She didn't want Saman to go with her and that dreadful pansy husband of hers to Luxor. Thank God I insisted. I said I wouldn't go without Saman. She relented but with bad grace.'

'I don't know why you dislike Oliver. I find him good company and amusing.'

'He shows his hatred of woman,' said Joan with feeling. 'So did you, at first. Now you're all right.'

'Thank you,' returned Ronald. 'I think that Oliver doesn't intend to appear antagonistic. He's shy. What about Khalid? Do you like him?'

'He seems OK. I haven't thought about him much.'

'He's mad about you.'

'I thought he was gay, being your friend.'

'No, he's not gay. He does "it" with me to oblige,' Ronald confessed.

Joan refilled the teacups, and then said, 'I think I'm in love with Saman.'

'He's attractive, but it wouldn't be very practical to marry. The two cultures, his and yours, are so different.'

'Practical! What a word to use! Difference in upbringing and cultures don't matter. Were both human beings. You're a cold fish, aren't you, Ronald? Romance isn't in your vocabulary.'

Ronald bridled. 'Well, I don't know about that.'

Simultaneously they raised their cups to their lips and sipped. Putting down his cup, Ronald asked, 'What did you think of Suez?'

'Well, you were there with us—'

'No, no, I meant the Suez campaign in 1956 when British and French troops invaded Port Said. Dropped bombs.'

'In 1956,' Joan replied, 'I was thirteen. I don't remember much about it.'

'I was in the Lebanon as I once told you. I was 38. I was so incensed by the invasion that I wrote to my MP in England and I like to think as a result he voted against the campaign. Eden's "We are going to separate the combatants" was a barefaced lie. The Israelis hadn't yet reached the Canal. I felt ashamed. The British bombed my favourite hotel in Port Said – the Eastern Exchange; a marvellous name, a relic of the days when civil servants and hopeful maidens went to India on P&O liners, the days of "port out and starboard home", the days of an emporium called Simon Artz that sold among a host of things wonderful Egyptian cigarettes. One bought them by the hundred in a pink box. How good they were!'

'But you don't smoke.'

'I did then. Most people smoked then. It was before the American Surgeon General's devastating and convincing report connecting smoking with lung cancer and heart disease.'

'Simon Artz sounds Jewish.'

'It was. I'm talking of the days in Egypt when the Muslims and the Jews tolerated each other. Before the creation of Israel, before Egypt felt threatened.'

'When was this?'

'In the war, the Second World War. I was in the army in Egypt.'

'You go back a long way.'

'Not so very long,' replied Ronald, indignantly.

☪

Cedric was a man of fixed habits. His days in Cairo fell into a routine, which he found perfectly supportable. He had to work late in the offices of the newspaper, but that suited him because he didn't have to start work until after lunch. He had no desire for a social existence. Lunch with Ronald once or twice a week was all he required in the way of contact with a fellow countryman. His work on the paper precluded him from his having any evening appointments. In the office he was friendly with and courteous to his colleagues, and he felt he was more than just tolerated by them. He got on with his work steadily and efficiently, sitting at his desk and editing articles brought to him by junior members of the staff. As in Baghdad, the leaders Cedric wrote were about non-political subjects, such as the development of a new province, or the problem of how to preserve Abu Simbel when the waters of Lake Nasser would threaten to submerge the temple. As regards his sex life, Cedric kept quiet about it, although there wasn't much for inquisitive eyes to discover. Apart from his peeping at the boy in the bookshop, and allowing his middle-aged servant, a father of five, to get into his bed on two mornings a week there was nothing to reveal.

Cedric wasn't paid much more than the average staff writer and therefore had to be parsimonious. He didn't mind this; in fact he liked carefully budgeting his expenditure. His mother had left him around £50,000 and her small flat in Worthing had sold for a similar sum; he had put the money into British government stock and never touched the interest. 'For my old age,' he told himself; he was nearly a sexagenarian. A visiting BBC reporter contacted him one day and suggested he make a radio programme about local life for the World Service. Cedric agreed.

He made a programme about a café near the opera house. The proprietor spoke English quite well and he willingly cooperated. He arranged a recording session with Cedric and those of the café's regular customers who were willing to answer the questions that Cedric posed in his rather basic Arabic and then translated into English. He sent the tape to the

BBC and when he was informed of the time of the broadcast he arranged with the proprietor to alert the regular customers who gathered round a small Sony transistor set and listened with delight to the sound of their voices coming from London. The success of the broadcast brought requests from the BBC World Service for further programmes. Cedric made one on the port of Alexandria, the recently discovered tombs for bulls at Sakkara, and on the railway museum. These broadcasts gave Cedric a fillip and made him feel that he was doing something for Anglo-Egyptian relations by showing a side of Egypt that wasn't connected with politics and hostility.

☪

Ronald's forgetting his camera on the day of the Suez trip with Khalid resulted in the young man knowing where Ronald and Joan lived at Nile College. One afternoon Khalid went out to Maadi and found the way to the College and the foreigners' residence. Ronald's car was not outside. Khalid ascended the stairs to the first floor and knocked at a door on the left of the hall.

'Come in,' cried Joan's voice.

Khalid entered. Joan was having tea in the little sitting-room.

'Hello,' she said. 'Ronald's gone into Cairo.'

Khalid stood gazing at her.

Joan said, 'Would you like a cup of tea?'

'Yes,' replied Khalid, who seemed confused.

'Well, sit down then. I'll freshen this up.' She took the teapot into the kitchen. On her return, she found the young Egyptian still on his feet. 'Do sit down,' she said in her teacher's voice. Khalid remained standing and staring.

'Won't you have a cup of tea?' asked Joan.

'Yes,' Khalid said, but instead of sitting down he moved round the table towards her. 'Miss Jo-an, I love you.'

'Oh Lord!'

He put a hand on her shoulder. She didn't move and soon she found herself in his arms. 'Miss Jo-an,' he sighed, 'I love you.'

'Don't be silly.' She felt his strong prick against her body; it seemed much bigger than Saman's.

'What about Ronald?' she asked.

'No matter,' he replied, holding her fast and pressing himself against her. 'You no have bed?'

'Yes,' she said, her voice shaking.

'Where?'

'In here.' She led the way into the bedroom.

Khalid pushed her on to the bed and lay on top of her. She didn't protest. This violent, rape-like vigour excited her. She relaxed and let him pull her clothes apart; quickly he divested himself of his sweater, shirt, trousers and underpants. 'A fine figure of a man,' she said to herself, admiring his broad shoulders and muscular arms. 'I can see why Ronald likes him. I suppose gays go for manly men with big things. It's puzzling to know what Khalid sees in him, or, it seems in Oliver. Only money?'

In making love Khalid had none of the gentleness or consideration of Saman, but the thrusts of his robust penis made her moan in ecstasy. He was soon finished.

'*Hamman* you have?'

'In there.' Joan indicated the bathroom door. 'I hope the water's hot.' Khalid took some of his garments into the bathroom with him. She supposed that the water was hot as he didn't reappear. She was glad she had gone on taking precautions after Saman had left. Lying back in bed, she thought about Saman, Violet and now Khalid. Saman and Violet were rich and had the self-assurance that wealth bestows and at the same time protects them from the rough edges of life. Joan found Saman's oriental outlook fascinating. She felt she would never know him completely. Does one know anyone completely? Violet, of course, was easier to know than the Chinese Thai and with her Joan felt safe, and she could not give her children, yet Saman's exoticism had a depth that was so enticing.

Khalid entered the bedroom wearing his underpants and his shirt.

'What about Ronald?' she asked.

'Ronald?' Khalid inquired as if he had never heard of him.

'Yes, Ronald, or Ron as you call him,' she replied in a tone of impatience. 'Your friend Ron. He won't be pleased, will he?'

Khalid stepped into his trousers. 'No matter.'

'Will you tell him?'

'I not tell.' He poked his head into his sweater and pulled it down each side, and then smoothed his short, wiry hair.

'I'll tell him,' said Joan wickedly; she meant this as a joke.

Khalid's answer surprised her. 'As you like,' he said.

'No, of course I won't.'

'Goodbye, Miss Jo-an.' Khalid held out a hand which she, still in bed, took. He left the flat without showing any tenderness towards her.

She felt he had used her like a prostitute and yet she had to admit it had been exciting. She did not wish to repeat it although she knew she would often think about it. Was it shameful to have enjoyed what Ronald enjoyed, to have sort of cuckholded him? It gave her a perverse pleasure to have known the body of Ronald's and Oliver's paramour; her new knowledge gave her a sort of power over them, made her feel superior; after all, same-sex sex wasn't as satisfactory as hetero-sex. She was sure that Khalid only had sex with Ronald and Oliver as they were kind to him and paid him. They were *fautes de mieux*. She was what Khalid really wanted. She revelled in the thought. She was glad that Saman was normal. Was the need of money the only reason that Khalid had it off with middle-aged men? Would Saman, if poor, be like Khalid? No, the Arabs were different. They were obsessed about the chastity of their women and before marriage had to look for other outlets.

☪

Cedric was half way through his omelette and his glass of red wine was almost empty, when Violet and Oliver joined him with a 'Do you mind?' from Oliver.

Violet announced, 'I've just returned from Assuyt.'

'Your Coptic studies continue then,' said Cedric. 'At the moment it's not the Copts who are in the news but the Arab-Israeli situation. It's boiling up. All sorts of menaces are being exchanged and there are border raids especially across the Syrian and Jordanian frontiers.'

'Will all this come to anything?' asked Oliver, anxiously.

'Did you know that the Copts often suffer persecution?' asked Violet.

'Never mind the Copts, dear,' said Oliver. 'The Arab-Israeli confrontation is much more important. Cedric, do you think we ought to go?'

'I don't think much will happen here,' he replied. 'But things might get nasty. Nasser has said he will attack Israel if they don't stop their taunts.'

'But isn't their army in the Yemen?' asked Oliver.

'Not all of it.'

'But Israel is tough, well-armed, thanks to the Americans.'

'It's all threats and shouting at the moment,' explained Cedric. 'It may come to nothing.'

'Let's hope so,' said Oliver.

'I must go to Fayoum,' said Violet, who seemed unconcerned about the threat of war. 'There is an important Coptic church there, and then I must visit Wadi Natrun to see the monasteries.'

'There may be convents too, darling,' suggested Oliver.

☪

Towards the middle of May euphoria broke out in Cairo. The Egyptian army started to move across the Suez Canal into Sinai to take up positions on the frontier with Israel. Now that the UN observers had been requested to withdraw the two enemies faced one another.

Posters ridiculing Israel and the USA appeared all over the Egyptian capital. Some of them were pathetically childish: a long-nosed Uncle Sam piloting a plane descending in flames, shot down by a triumphant Egyptian fighter pilot; a number of heavily-armed Israeli soldiers burdened by huge proboscises were fleeing from an Arab boy with a catapult; an Israeli being kicked in the air by an Egyptian footballer. There were small anti-Israeli and anti-American demonstrations in the city centres. There was an atmosphere of excitement and optimism in the air. People seemed confident that war with Israel would be a pushover.

☪

Ronald was surprised when Khalid said he wanted to be taken to Port Said.
'Why?'
'I want buy a shirt.'
'A shirt?'
'There are good cheap shirts that shops get from foreign ships.'
As usual Ronald acceded to his friend's wishes.
They set off in Ronald's car, which Khalid, who had no licence, wanted to drive, but, as at the start of the Suez trip, Ronald firmly did not allow him to do so. Halfway to Ismailia they stopped to watch a training exercise. From a raised platform, about fifty foot high, soldiers were being made to jump into the sweet water canal that ran alongside the road. On the platform was a soldier in a state of hesitation. A sergeant shouted at him to jump. The soldier stood on the edge of the platform, looked down and stepped back. He obeyed the command to try again and when he got to the edge, the sergeant gave him a push and emitting a yell of fear he dropped into the murky, bilharzia-ridden water. Ronald felt sorry for him and also for the soldiers he saw in the backs of trucks hurtling towards the Suez Canal. They looked unwarlike and unaggressive; simple *fellaheen* most of them, not very bright; their bravado was not convincing.

Ronald and Khalid drove through the dull little town of Ismailia and a few miles further north they were held up at Kantara while an Egyptian armoured brigade crossed the pontoon bridge into Sinai. Khalid was impressed. 'How can the Israelis stand up to this?' he said.

They drove on alongside the Canal, passing oil tanker after oil tanker. Ronald told Khalid the countries the ships belonged to. Many of them flew the Norwegian flag.

'This Norway,' said Khalid, 'is big country?'

'No, but it has many ships.'

'*Ya salaam!*'

Ronald had not been to Port Said for several years. The streets that were bombed during the Suez campaign had been partly rebuilt. Alas, his favourite hotel, the Eastern Exchange, had gone. They put up at the Casino Palace a pre-World War II establishment that had lost its grandeur.

☪

Oliver was lunching alone in Groppi's. When he saw Cedric enter the restaurant, he waved and the newspaper man joined him.

Oliver said, 'Violet has taken the car and gone to Wadi Natrun with a Coptic priest from a church near the Coptic museum. She left this morning oblivious to the threat of war.'

'Also oblivious to the threat of war is Ronald. He's gone off to Port Said with Khalid.'

'Oh has he?' Oliver turned back to his *veau pané* with *pommes purées* and cut a slice of meat in two and forked one of the pieces into his mouth. While chewing, he looked at Cedric. 'Tell me about the situation.'

'It's becoming serious. Nasser seems determined to help Syria, which is undergoing provocative raids by the Israeli army.'

'D'you think we should leave?'

'You have no reason to stay,' replied Cedric.

'Except that I can't get in touch with Violet. I can hardly leave without her.'

'The monastries are very remote. They wouldn't be affected if Egypt were invaded.'

'But what about my car and my wife? I told Violet that it was madness to take the Jaguar on rough desert roads, especially after that breakdown outside Suez. She gave me the car for my birthday but she still regards it as hers. What's going to happen, d'you think?'

'I don't know.'

'But you're a newspaperman. You should know or have a good idea anyway.'

'I think nothing will happen. It's just sabre-rattling.'

'I hope you're right, Cedric.'

☪

Nile College was in the midst of exams. Ronald had managed to take two days off, but Joan was invigilating in the dining-hall, which held about half the school. The pupils were at the moment more concerned with writing answers than with the situation, while she was full of worries. Saman hadn't written; there was the possibility of war with Israel; what would happen?; she had rung Violet, spoken to Oliver, who had told her his wife had left for Wadi Natrun, Joan was puzzled by this sudden fascination of Violet's for the Coptic Church; and Khalid, would he appear again? Had he told Ronald? She hadn't; if she had to go, would the Ministry of Education pay her fare back to Britain? Joan felt distraught.

While patrolling the aisles she spotted a student, one of hers, copying from a crib. She pounced and tried to seize the crib, but the boy held on to it and it tore in half. 'This nothing,' said the boy. She called the senior invigilator over. An argument pursued. 'He says he wasn't cheating,' the invigilator told Joan. 'But he was,' insisted Joan. 'Let us tear this up and then he can't cheat anymore, if he was cheating,' said the invigilator, reducing the piece of paper to confetti. Joan's demand for the boy to be dismissed was ignored. Furious, she left the room apologising to Mr Thomas, who was looking downcast. He had two sons: one at a university, the other in a secondary school. He was afraid of their being called up into the army. 'The situation is not good, Miss Joan,' he remarked gloomily.

Joan went back to her flat to find under her door had been pushed a letter from the British Consul advising all British residents to leave Egypt, unless their work was essential.

What was she to do?

☪

Ronald and Khalid were lolling in deck chairs on the beach near the Casino Palace. Khalid seemed quite unconcerned about the situation. He was more interested in the shirts he had bought from some shady shop a friend had told him about. He had brought them down from the hotel to show Ronald.

'But they're so thick, Khalid.'

'Very fashion.'

The shirts were woollen with tartan designs, more suitable for a lumberjack than a Cairene banker. Ronald looked at the labels. 'Made in Canada,' he read. 'They'll be rather hot. Perhaps all right for the winter.'

'They are good.'

'I should think they'll wear well, last a long time.'

They lolled in the sun for the rest of the afternoon: Khalid dozing, Ronald reading.

That night when they were in bed together, Khalid confessed to Ronald about his having had sex with Joan.

'What an unfaithful boy you are! You're oversexed, that's your trouble. There's Oliver and now Joan. Did you enjoy it with Joan?'

'Not so very.'

'Why did you do it?'

'I want see what she like.'

'I can understand that. Sexual curiosity is quite usual. How naughty you are!'

'You don't mind, Mister Ron.'

'It's a bit late for me to mind, Khalid.'

'You not angry with me? I come Maadi to see you. You not there, so I speak with Miss Joan and she invite me into her room and she make me do it.'

Ronald guessed he was lying, but he didn't challenge him. 'No, I'm not angry, but don't do it again.'

'I never, Mister Ron.'

The next day they motored back to Cairo. Ronald dropped Khalid off at Tahrir Square and motored on to Nile College.

☪

Hearing Ronald's car arrive, Joan hurried out of her apartment to meet Ronald as he gained the first floor.

'We've got to go,' she said, apprehensively.

'Where?'

'To leave. There's a letter from the British Consul advising British residents to leave.'

'Because of the situation?'

'Yes.'

'Cairo seemed normal. The Canal was functioning as usual. I've just come back from Port Said.'

'Read the letter. There's one for you.'

Ronald picked up his letters from the hall table and at once opened the one from the Consul. 'Should we leave, do you think?'

'You know better than I,' replied Joan.

'I'll ask Cedric. I'm seeing him tomorrow.'

'Shouldn't we decide now?'

There came a cry from the front door, followed by hasty steps on the stairs and there entered Oliver and Hassan, one of Ronald's most attractive and ill-behaved pupils.

'Oliver!' exclaimed Ronald. 'How did you find us?'

'I took a taxi to the College and this young man kindly showed me where you lived.'

Hassan gave a huge, roguish grin.

'Thank you, Hassan,' said Ronald, dismissively.

'Ah, thank you very much,' said Oliver, reaching for his wallet.

'No, no,' said Ronald, 'not necessary.'

Hassan's face fell and after shaking hands with Oliver left.

'Why did you come by taxi? Has your car broken down again?' asked Ronald.

'No, it hasn't. Violet is still away in Wadi Natrun with the car. What are we going to do?' Oliver was agitated.

'About what?' asked Ronald, knowing what Oliver was referring to.

'About the situation, about leaving. I've seen the Consul and he advised leaving. But I can't leave without the car and without Violet, can I?'

Ronald was about to say, 'Why not?', but he substituted, 'I suppose not.'

Joan said, 'Of course you can't.'

'She's become obsessed with the Copts. Violet gets these obsessions with causes and with people.'

Joan blushed.

☪

'As I told Oliver, I don't think anything will happen,' Cedric said to Ronald, over the lunch table in Groppi's.

'Joan wants to go. She's never liked it here. She's dying to get back to Saman, who's still in England.'

'What about you, Ronald?'

'I don't want to go, but perhaps I should. I don't fancy staying here if there's going to be panic and turmoil.'

'How would you go?'

'By car. I'd drive to Libya and then on to Tunisia, thence a boat to Marseilles.'

'What about Khalid?'

'I'm fond of him of course, but he's never pulled my heart strings strongly; after all he's been to bed with Oliver, and with Joan, so he told me when we were in Port Said.'

'What about Violet?'

'I'm sure he hasn't been to bed with her.'

'No, I meant, does she want to leave?'

'I don't know. Oliver does. He's quite nervous about the situation. Anyway Violet's Oliver's business, not mine. It's amusing that when Oliver mentions Violet he puts the car first. I suppose she'll be safe out at Wadi Natrun.'

'Coptic monks can be sexy,' remarked Cedric.

'Is there a convent there? Violet would prefer a nun to a monk.'

'I don't know.'

'What are you going to do, Cedric? Will you leave?'

'I can't. I have a job and I've nowhere to go anyway. When will you decide?'

'After lunch.'

☪

Ronald and Joan saw the headmaster together and told him they had been advised to leave. Although neither of them had been an outstanding success at Nile College, the headmaster was disappointed that his two foreign teachers wished to leave; perhaps their presence gave the school some prestige (they were both academically qualified) and their performances in their classrooms didn't matter.

Ronald had agreed to take Joan to Tripoli in his car, from there she would fly to London and he would motor on to Tunis. He did not relish the thought of driving the six hundred miles alone, and Joan, after all, was sensible and bearable company; although she couldn't drive, at least she could see that he didn't fall asleep at the wheel.

The next few days were spent in hurried preparations for departure. They both had to queue for over an hour among a milling crowd of fellow applicants for exit visas in the government building in Tahrir Square. Joan's blonde presence was a help. She caught the eye of one of the officials and he stretched out his arm and took her and Ronald's passports to the annoyance of other applicants.

☪

Oliver was in a deep state of worry and distress over not having any news about the Jaguar or Violet and deciding whether he should leave them. When he saw the British Consul again his concern was not assuaged.

'I can't leave without my wife,' Oliver said to the Consul, a tall, youngish man with a monocle and an upper-class accent that didn't quite ring true.

'I suppose not,' said the Consul.

'It wouldn't be much use my going to Wadi Natrun in search of her, would it?'

'I suppose not.'

'What do you advise then?'

'It's up to you.'

When Oliver had walked the short distance from the Embassy to the Semiramis, he was much relieved to see the Jaguar parked outside the hotel. He hastened up to his suite. Violet was in the bath. 'You're back!' Oliver shouted outside the bathroom door.

'Yes.'

'How was it?'

'I'll tell you when I'm dressed.'

Later, in the sitting-room, Violet related to her husband her adventures at Wadi Natrun. She had found the various monasteries and their works of religious art of great interest, but there was no decent accomodation available. 'In a word,' said Violet, 'the place is squalid. I'm not sorry I went there. I feel though one can learn as much, perhaps more, about the Copts from books than from a visit. What news of Joan?'

'I hear that she and Ronald are taking the Consul's advice to leave and he is going to drive her to Libya.'

'What!' exclaimed Violet both alarmed and astonished.

'To Libya. To Tripoli, from where she can get a plane to London.'

'Can't she get a flight from here?'

'I don't know. It's a long drive, not one to do alone. She's going in order to keep him company.'

'Oh is she? Where is she now?'

'At Nile College, I suppose. Packing.'

'I'll go and see her.' Violet took up her handbag from the occasional table.

'I'll come with you. I know the way. I went there recently.' Oliver rose from his armchair.

'No. I prefer to go alone.' Violet made for the door, stopped and turned. 'Why did you go to Nile College?' she asked suspiciously.

'To see Ronald. To find out what he and Joan were going to do about the Consul's advice to leave.'

☪

Violet arrived at Nile College around lunchtime. The pupils were wandering about, some kicking a football, others chatting in groups. When the Jaguar drew up it was immediately surrounded by inquisitive boys.

'May I help you?' asked one of them.

'Please can you tell me where Miss Joan Webber lives?'

'I show you,' said Hassan.

'Thank you.'

Although it would have been easy to direct Violet to the house, Hassan, pleased to show off in front of his classmates, got into the passenger seat and waved to them as if he was off on a journey. They soon arrived at the house. Ronald's little Fiat was parked outside.

Hassan jumped out and opened Violet's door.

'Thank you,' she said.

'It upstair. I show you.'

They mounted the stairs together and came upon Ronald and Joan in the hall. They appeared to be having an altercation.

'No really, Joan, I can't take all that. There's my stuff too, you know.'

'You could get a rack put on the roof,' Joan suggested.

'It would make my car top-heavy.'

'Maybe I could help,' said Violet.

The two turned round.

'Violet!' exclaimed Joan.

'Back from Wadi Natrun?' Ronald said lamely. 'Thank you, Hassan. You're proving to be useful, for once.'

Hassan left.

'That wasn't a very nice thing to say to the young man, was it?' remarked Violet. 'He was charming and helpful.'

'You don't know him. In class, he can be a pest.'

Violet addressed Joan. 'I hear you two are leaving together.'

Before Joan had time to reply, Ronald put in, 'Joan has kindly offered to accompany me to Tripoli. It's a six-hundred mile drive, mostly across desert.'

'But he can't take all my things,' whined Joan.

'That's easily solved,' said Violet. 'There's plenty of room in my car. You can come with us.'

'Are you going to Libya too then?' asked Ronald.

'Well, we can. Oliver thinks we should leave. I'll tell him. Joan, I've never seen your rooms.'

Joan took the hint and giving Ronald an apologetic glance took Violet into her flat. Ronald didn't follow them.

'Oh Joan,' said Violet, 'it's so good to see you. I've missed you so.'

'How was Wadi Natrun?' Joan asked, not wishing to talk about their relationship.

'Interesting,' replied Violet. 'But darling, I want to talk about us.'

'*Us*?' repeated Joan, knitting her eyebrows, feigning puzzlement.

'You and me,' said Violet, irritably.

'It would be more constructive if we talked about Saman and me. I love him.'

'Rubbish. Infatuated is what you mean. Nothing can be built out of infatuation, it's made of flimsy material. He's exotic with his oriental eyes and raven hair, I admit. But you could never have a lasting relationship with him. Oriental husbands are notoriously irresponsible and promiscuous. I can offer you so much, Joan.'

Joan took a breath and braced herself. 'What do you know about oriental husbands? He can offer me more.'

Violet gave Joan a wondering look. 'I suppose he can, in a way,' she said. 'Well, that's neither here nor there at the moment. Let's talk about going to Libya.'

☪

The school was often late in paying the monthly salaries which were, at the end of May, now due. Ronald went over to the College cashier and was pleasantly surprised to be handed his money in an envelope. 'No hope of a travel allowance,' he said to the cashier, an oldish and kindly man, who sadly shook his head. 'You are not entitled to it as you were locally employed,' he told Ronald. 'You could apply but to get it would mean putting in an application, and you know what happens to applications in this country.'

'Well, never mind.' Ronald bid the cashier, a gentle man he liked, goodbye. He wasn't responsible for the overweighted Egyptian bureaucracy that functioned like an antiquated machine which constantly broke down and took an age to repair unless the wheels were oiled by a bribe or blonde features like Joan's. Joan got her money and also her fare home. Since she had been on a year's contract and engaged from abroad, by some fluke the money had come through. Ronald was envious.

He went into Cairo, where he asked for some dollars from a small shop that sold tobacco and newspapers and whose owner acted as a clandestine moneychanger. While the owner went off somewhere to procure the American money, Ronald chatted to his teenage son, who was sitting on a low stool and reading a newspaper.

'What will you do, if there's a war?' Ronald asked.

'I fight.'

'You will join the army?'

'Yes, to fight.'

There was a photograph of Nasser in the paper. The boy hit the photo with his fist. 'I fight for him and for Egypt. I love him.'

The dollars, which were sold to him at an inflated rate, arrived. Ronald thanked the owner of the shop for his illicit services and joined Cedric at Groppi's.

'So you're off, Ronald.'

'Yes. The idea is for the Brents, Joan and me to go together to Libya.'

'You'll leave your car here?'

'No. We'll go in two cars.'

'A convoy,' sneered Cedric. 'To leave at this time of the year is sensible; it's beginning to get hot. But to run away because of the war scare is as pusillanimous as it is unnecessary. Nothing will happen except skirmishing in the Sinai desert. The Arabs love a scrap, so long as it is not much more than a sort of bedouin raid. If Israel didn't exist they'd be at each other's throats.' He paused to fork a potato chip into his mouth. 'What will you do when you get back to Merrie England?'

'Try and negotiate a job in Japan,' replied Ronald. 'That's where I've been happiest – Japan.'

'So you won't be coming this way again?'

'Unlikely.'

'What about Joan?'

'She'll shack up with Saman in Bangkok, I imagine, provided she's not devoured by Violet.'

'Violet,' Cedric repeated the name. 'What'll happen to the Brents?'

'Nothing. They'll go on acting out their whims. They can afford to.'

After the meal the two friends bid each other goodbye.

Ronald went to say farewell to the landlord of his hutch in Bab-el-Louk, collected a few oddments from his rooms – pajamas, towels, underwear, shaving things, a toothbrush, letters, envelopes and half a bottle of Greek brandy – and put them in his car. He suddenly remembered that Khalid was due the next evening. He wrote a note explaining his departure, put twenty Egyptian pounds in an envelope and asked the *bawab*, a Sudanese in flowing white jellaba to give the letter to Khalid.

'I will say my prayers at the door and know when he comes,' said the doorman. Ronald gave him five pounds and received warm thanks and wishes that Allah would protect him.

☪

Outside the flats at Nile College a bunch of boys had gathered to watch Ronald and Joan leave. Violet and Oliver had arrived in their Jaguar.

Joan appeared with two suitcases; a boy rushed forward to help her.

'It would be better to put those in my car,' said Violet, 'There's more room in my car than in Ronald's. I have a huge boot.'

Joan allowed the boy to take her suitcases and Violet supervised the loading of them. 'I have two more,' she confessed.

'Never mind. We can get them in. Oliver hasn't much. Two of his bags can go in Ronald's car.' Oliver stood idly by watching and now and then eyeing Hassan, who was one of the bunch of boys.

Ronald appeared. 'Hassan,' he called from the front door of the building, 'come and help and bring two others.' Hassan threw Oliver a glance and obeyed Ronald's command.

When all the baggage had been brought down, Ronald stood aside and let Violet organize the loading of it, which she did efficiently, directing the boys with authority and decision. He realized her plan before she announced it herself. 'Now Oliver, you go with Ronald and Joan you come with me.

Joan hesitated before getting into the passenger seat of the Jaguar. Oliver regarded Ronald, who was standing apart with Hassan and chatting to him. And then after friendly handshakes, all were aboard and then with cries of goodbye from the boys, the cars moved off, the Jaguar leading.

☪

'We haven't decided which way we're going to Alexandria,' said Ronald to Oliver. The desert way or the Delta way. Nor did we arrange to meet in Alex.'

'We won't see them again,' replied Oliver. 'Violet made a sly plan to kidnap Joan.'

'It's just as well,' added Ronald. 'I like her, but I'd much rather have you as a companion; besides, you can help with the driving.'

Oliver laughed. 'That's why you prefer my company, is it? By the way, what were you saying to the beautiful Hassan just before we left?'

'Just goodbye. D'you know what he said? He said, "Don't go away. You come stay my house. When all over we kill you." He ran a finger across his throat and gave his engaging smile. Once in class he stood up and said, "Sir, what is cock?" "The masculine of hen," I replied. "Sir, I think it have other meaning," went on Hassan. "I'll tell you after the class." "Tell me now, sir, please sir." "No." "Is it what I make water with?" "Yes, now sit down." "Sir," Hassan persisted, "English boy say to me 'take my cock', now I know I kill him."'

They both laughed.

'He's attractive,' remarked Oliver.

'Yes,' agreed Ronald,' but he's a devil in class. He reads magazines under his desk. He talks. He never does his homework.'

'Did you punish him?'

'Not really.'

'Would you punish him if he were ugly?'

'I treat everyone the same, girls or boys, ugly or beautiful.'

'Is Hassan queer?'

'No, I'm sure he isn't; he's just young and lusty. The Egyptians are not really queer, just sexy; they have a ready prick. There are Egyptian queers, but they're frightfully effeminate.'

'What about Khalid?'

'He falls into the "just sexy" category.'

'I would have liked to have said goodbye to him and given him a present, but I was so caught up with the problem about leaving and Violet being away in Wadi Natrun on her crazy Coptic studies.'

'He was coming to see me tonight. I left him twenty pounds in an envelope which I gave to the *bawab* to give him. I hope he will. I think he will. I felt I could trust him. He's Sudanese. A fine man.'

They had reached Tahrir Square. 'I think I'll take the desert road,' said Ronald. 'It's longer but it's not cluttered with carts, water buffalo, trucks, buses, cars and—'

'People,' added Oliver.

'Yes people, people wandering about oblivious to everything.'

Ronald took the bridge across the Nile and then the way to the Pyramids and so on to the desert road to Alexandria.

☪

'I think we'll go by the Delta road,' Violet said to Joan. 'It's quicker.'

'What about the others?' asked Joan.

'They'll look after themselves.'

'We haven't arranged to meet them anywhere.'

'We'll run into them, I expect,' said Violet.

'Where are we going to spend the night?'

'They told me at the Semiramis that there's a resort hotel by the sea near el Alamein. We ought to get there in time for dinner.'

'Again I ask,' said Joan, insistently, 'what about the others?'

'Again I reply, they're able to look after themselves. They're birds of a feather, you know.'

☪

'We're nearing Alex,' said Ronald. 'I suggest we put up at the Hotel Cecil.'

'The Cecil! That takes me back. Is it still going?'

'Yes. I went there last year with Khalid.'

'You never told me.'

'Didn't I? It was before you and Violet arrived. We had a rest in our room after we'd checked in, and we found a bed-bug in our bed. I complained to one of the receptionists on our way out to dinner and he said, looking at Khalid, who was standing nearby, "Some people bring in bedbugs with their luggage."'

'How monstrous! And you recommend the Cecil?'

'It's the only hotel I know and it's convenient.'

'Why did you take Khalid to Alexandria? asked Oliver, jealous.

'He wanted to buy a briefcase and he'd heard that one could get good, cheap ones there. We went from shop to shop but he didn't like any of the ones we were shown. I got very fed up and said, "Let's get that one", and he turned to me with a look of disapproval and said, "Mister Ron, that not good shopping." I didn't realize that the Egyptians enjoy shopping around without purchasing anything. We came away without getting a briefcase. Last week I took him to Port Said, as I told you. He had heard that one could get good shirts there. Having suffered the experience of Egyptian-style shopping in Alex, in Port Said I let him go shirt-hunting on his own. He bought three woollen shirts made in Canada, which were quite unsuitable for Egypt. But they were foreign and in spite of their policy the Egyptians like foreign things.'

They had reached the city and carefully negotiating the way through the clutter of traffic, Ronald drove past the docks to Maidan Said Zaghlul where the Hotel Cecil stood. Inside the atmosphere was seedy and the doormen seemed annoyed at having to attend to the arrivals' luggage; the receptionists were equally offhand.

☪

The arrival of Violet and Joan at the resort hotel near el Alamein was different from that of Oliver and Ronald at the Cecil. The two women were welcomed warmly and willing hands belonging to turbooshed servants in white jellabas dealt with the luggage.

At the reception desk Violet firmly asked for one double room. Jane said, 'I feel very tired, Violet. I think I'd rather have a room on my own.'

Violet ignored Joan's request and their bags were taken up to a room with one double-bed in it.

The hotel was empty and the two women dined alone and mostly in silence while eating the table d'hôte menu, whose redeeming item was the lentil soup which Violet declined.

'Don't you like lentil soup?' asked Joan.

'It's too heavy, too fattening.'

'With *fool* – beans – it's Egypt's best dish.'

'Beans are not for me,' said Violet, haughtily.

Later after consuming the *poulet chasseur*, Joan again broke the silence by saying, 'I wonder what's happened to the others.'

'I wonder,' replied Violet, as if their fate was of no concern to her.

☪

'Let's dine at the Union,' suggested Ronald.

'Is it still going?' asked Oliver. 'I remember it in the war.'

'We can walk there.'

At the restaurant they both chose red mullet preceded by lentil soup, and they ordered a bottle of Clos Mariut.

'Did you know Bill Heddington?' asked Ronald.

'I may have done. I can't remember.'

'He had a flat in Cairo and told his servant to serve lentil soup every night.'

'I'm fond of lentil soup,' said Oliver, 'but I wouldn't want it every night.'

'What about *fool?*'

'The beans?'

'Yes. The Coptic ladies who run the Felfela restaurant in Cairo produce marvellous *fool medani*. Did you take Violet there?'

'No. Violet might have liked the place because of the Coptic ladies. I wonder what's happened to our two ladies.'

'I wonder,' said Ronald taking a sip of the white wine. Showing his nonchalance, he added, 'I think I prefer this to the red.'

'Omar Khayam, you mean. It's funny that the Egyptians name one of their wines after a Persian poet.'

☪

The next morning Violet insisted on starting early. Joan wanted to stay in bed. 'Are we in a hurry?' she asked. She knew that Violet was in a bad mood because she had resisted the older woman's advances during the night.

'We must get into Libya as soon as possible in case war breaks out.'

'The staff seemed very relaxed about the situation, and those maintenance men we spoke to seemed quite cheerful,' went on Joan.

'They *seemed* to be. I think they were deeply worried,' insisted Violet.

'They talked of how they were looking forward to the summer season and then going to Upper Egypt for the winter.'

'Sheer Arab optimism,' said Violet scornfully. 'Look Joan, we decided to take the Consul's advice and leave the country. So we must do so as quickly as possible. Come on, girl, for God's sake.'

☪

'I wonder what Forster's tram conductor was like,' mused Oliver.

'I believe there's a studio photograph of him,' replied Ronald. 'He's sitting down, wearing a tarboosh, an ill-fitting jacket with a bow-tie -studio clothes, perhaps – and he has his forearm on a side table and holding a fly whisk, a sort of *effendi's* badge.'

'Attractive?'

'Fairly. Very solemn. But then that's usual. They rarely smile when photographed.'

Oliver was at the wheel of the Fiat. They were passing through the suburbs of Alex and aiming towards Mersa Matruh and Sollum on the Libyan frontier.

'This is very different from driving the Jag,' remarked Oliver.

'Sorry about that.'

'I don't mind, really. What about Cavafy? He lived in Alexandria like Forster's tram conductor.'

'He's a marvellous poet.'

'Yes, I know, but what about his queer life?'

'Most of his poems look back into the past. I love the one called "One Night".' Ronald cleared his throat and quoted, '"And there on the much-used lowly bed, I had the body of love, I had the—"'

'Talking of lowly beds,' interrupted Oliver, 'I saw one but never got into it.'

'Oh? Where was this?'

Oliver related his encounter with the male whore he picked up by the Nile.

'The walk by the river opposite the Hilton is infested with male whores. It was clever of you to throw the key across the floor and turn out the light.'

'I hoped it would skid under one of the beds,' said Oliver. 'One never learns. I left behind an expensive tie I bought at one of those cheating pseudo duty-free shops at an airport, so the wretched lad got something. One never learns. The strong urge one is cursed with leads to rashness. My God, this road is bumpy.'

They were nearing Mersa Matruh and seeing the sign to the resort hotel near el Alamein, Oliver said, 'Let's have have luncheon here. It's nearly one o'clock.' They had not risen early.

'OK, there's no need to rush. The frontier isn't far and if I know Egypt the Immigration and Customs people will take a nap after lunch.'

They were told by the hotel manager that two English ladies had spent the night in the establishment and had gone on to the frontier early that morning.

'I don't think we'll catch them up in your car,' said Oliver, disparagingly, during the meal.

'Does it matter if we don't?' asked Ronald.

'Well, Violet is my wife.'

'Wasn't it a *mariage de convenance?*'

'Yes, you could call it that. But when one has lived with someone for several years, a fondness develops.'

'Has she been jealous of your sexual exploits?' asked Ronald.

'Perhaps, a little. I certainly haven't been jealous of hers.'

'What about Khalid?'

'She met him several times. She never mentions him. I don't know what she thinks.'

'What do you think about Khalid?'

'He's wonderfully sexy. Just what I like.'

'Oh, really?'

☪

'It's surprising,' remarked Ronald when they had set out for Sollum, 'that there are no other cars. I thought there would be a queue of people escaping from Egypt.'

'Perhaps nothing will happen.'

At Sollum there were more donkeys than cars, most of which were registered in Libya, round the Immigration and Customs building, a block of concrete of no architectural merit. Sollum seemed to be a village with no streets, just sand with dwellings and offices scattered about as if tossed carelessly from the skies; the only redeeming feature of the forlorn place was the brilliant azure of the sea.

On a desiccated date palm hung a microphone which was booming out a speech by Nasser. The sonorous voice had to contend with much static and the hee-haws of the donkeys. Nasser was ranting against the British and the Americans. 'They are our enemies if they help Israel,' he said. He was giving a press conference in Cairo and sounded desperately tired. Ronald thought that Nasser's declaration was ominous and was pleased that he had decided to leave.

He and Oliver queued with a few other travellers including two Swedish girls hoping for a lift. At the Immigration office; their passports were stamped without demur, but the Customs official was more bureaucratic. Ronald had lost one of the car documents and one of the temporary Egyptian number plates had fallen off, but these delinquencies were waived after the payment of a fine. Ronald was then asked if he had any books.

'I have a number of books in my car.'

'Bring two of them.'

Ronald chose two books at random from the back of his car: an Everyman edition of Milton's poems and Pierre Loti's *Ramuntcho*; the latter bought at that bookshop from the naughty boy when the owner surprised them: Ronald remembered the occasion and hoped that the owner hadn't noticed anything. The book bore on the back of the cover the previous owner's name, a girl called Azisa Rajat.

'Your friend?' the official asked.

'No. A secondhand book.'

He gave Ronald a quizzical look and dismissed him with a nod. The two Swedish girls were behind and he had begun to notice them. They were pouting and looking glum and impatient.

Ronald and Oliver drove up the steep escarpment into Cyrenaica and took a last look at Sollum, now dolls-house size, the cars outside the Customs House resembled toys. 'Well, it's goodbye to Egypt,' Ronald said. 'Are you sorry?'

'Yes,' replied Oliver. 'I hate to run away, leave by the back door, as it were.'

'I agree. I shall always love Egypt.'

The sun was sinking fast and soon it was dark; no lights anywhere until they came upon King Idris's palace, the periphery of which was illuminated like a prison camp.

'Did you know Christopher Tower?' asked Ronald.

'No.'

'I've met him over the years here and there. At one time he was for a while political adviser to King Idris, who wanted to have Malik Idris in lights on the roof of his palace. Christopher managed to persuade the monarch that to do so would be vulgar, and the idea was abandoned. The King prefers the clean air of the desert to the corrupt, alien atmosphere in Tripoli. Oh, another thing I remember about Christopher. He had a Rolls Royce which the King coveted. Christopher in a wonderful Arab act of generosity gave it to him, much to the annnoyance of the British Embassy, none of whose staff could match such a grand gesture.'

'How splendid!' said Oliver.

The road was empty of traffic; the night was black.

After a long silence, Ronald, who was driving, said, 'Oliver, do you ever think of your schooldays. I do sometimes.'

'So do I.'

'When I think of schooldays, I think of the boys I had. I was mad about you, but we were in different houses and I was three years older than you. Do you remember that absurd unwritten rule about not fraternising with boys in another house?'

'Yes. Quite absurd,' concurred Oliver.

'It's funny how today one remembers those secret adventures. Our partners, whatever one calls them, were, of course, not queer, merely sexy, and now they're married and fathers and never think of those little moments of delight.'

'As we do,' agreed Oliver. 'Are we warped?'

'I suppose so,' returned Ronald. 'Do you remember the great scandal in my house when a boy sneaked, with the result that several boys were summarily expelled?'

'Yes, I do. And do you recall, Ronald, when the entire school were assembled and the headmaster announced that two boys had been found misbehaving behind a piano in one of the music rooms? I can hear his voice now saying, "I have had to write to their parents and ask them to remove the culprits. Do you realize what it was like to receive such a letter? It is like a Mills bomb on the breakfast table."'

They both laughed.

'The puritanical attitude towards sex,' said Ronald, 'in Britain is ridiculous, or used to be at any rate. Instead of a kindly counselling the offenders, they were chucked out forthwith. It was monstrous and showed a complete lack of understanding; after all boys in their late teens are in a highly sexual state.'

'Games and cold showers were supposed to quench their lust,' said Oliver.

'But they didn't.'

'Scratch an Englishman and you find a Puritan,' quipped Oliver. They drove on in silence for a while and then he asked, 'Are your parents dead?'

'Yes. I inherited what was left of their wealth, not much, but enough to keep my head above water between jobs.'

'My father died some time ago,' said Oliver, 'but my mother aged 89 is in a rest home which is slowly eating up her dwindling capital. When it runs out I shall have to ask Violet to help.'

'And will she?'

'Oh yes.'

☪

'I don't think you're in love with Saman,' Violet said.

'Oh, I am,' replied Joan. 'I think of him all the time.'

'It's merely a ploy to tease me.'

The two women had just left their hotel in Tobruk and were driving towards Benghazi. They were twelve hours ahead of Oliver and Ronald. Violet ignored Joan's suggestion that they should wait for the two men. Joan had managed so far to fend off Violet's attempts to make love to her.

'But you have enjoyed it with me,' Violet insisted.

'It was a new experience. One I had thought about, but never practised until I met you—'

'And,' interrupted Violet, 'there were fringe benefits?'

'Yes, you can put it that way, if you like.' Joan leaned forward in her seat and looked at the older woman, who was driving along the desolate road so capably. 'You see your life was so different from mine. I've told you about my dreary lower middle-class upbringing. Meeting you and Saman and some of the other foreign students gave me new vistas into new worlds.'

'Who gave you the best vista?' demanded Violet, clearly hoping Joan would say her.

'Saman,' Joan dared reply.

'Why?' snapped Violet.

'It's hard to define why one likes or loves someone. I find Saman attractive, and to be honest with myself and you, sexy. I find him exotic and excitingly mysterious—'

'Excitingly mysterious!' repeated Violet sarcastically. 'You sound like a guidebook to the orient.'

'It's true,' insisted Joan. 'I do find him exciting because he's different, his way of thinking and acting are unfathomable in a way. I like that.'

'We won't go to Cyrene,' said Violet. 'We'll go straight on to Benghazi.'

And straight on to Benghazi they went; and at the hotel in the second town of Libya they had separate bedrooms.

☪

'We *must* see the Temple of Apollo at Cyrene,' said Ronald to Oliver as they were about to get into their car. 'This is a marvellous opportunity.'

'Oh yes,' replied Oliver vaguely. Ronald guessed that Oliver had not heard of Cyrene, but he didn't challenge him.

They had spent the night in Tobruk in the same hotel at which Violet and Joan had stayed on the previous night; the staff, partly Greek, were uncooperative; no one helped with the luggage and the service at dinner and breakfast the next morning was indifferent.

'The trouble with an empty hotel or restaurant,' remarked Oliver, after they had moved off, 'is that the staff become idle and resent having to do anything.'

'What about Cyrene?' asked Ronald.

'What about it?'

'D'you want to visit the ruins?'

'Yes.'

'It will delay us.'

'Never mind.'

'We might spend the night there.'

'That's all right as far as I'm concerned. I'm not worried about Violet. We'll catch up with her eventually.'

'Why did she rush ahead like that?' asked Ronald.

'She wanted to be alone with Joan, of course.'

'Will she bed down with Joan?'

'If she can. She has done so before.'

'D'you mind?'

'Of course not.'

'But what if she eloped with Joan?'

'I might mind if she did that,' said Oliver. 'I depend on her, you know.'

'You're a kept boy,' taunted Ronald.

'Yes. I know I am. I despise myself for it sometimes, but the benefits outweigh the disadvantages. Violet and I agreed that for sex we could go our own ways, but we 'd live together. The arrangement has worked satisfactorily so far, but I find this abduction of Joan disturbing.'

'Shall we press on to Benghazi then and not go to Cyrene?' suggested Ronald.

'No, no, I'd like to see the place.'

'They motored on with Ronald at the wheel. At the top of the escarpment below which lay the ruins of the ancient city of Cyrene, Ronald paused. 'The descent looks very precipitous.'

'Would you like me to drive, Ronald?'

'No, thanks.'

'Go down in low gear,' Oliver advised.

'Yes, I know,' replied Ronald, petulantly.

At the bottom of the steep and twisting descent, they came across a small hotel.

The only person in evidence was a young Arab in shirt and jeans, who was sitting behind the reception desk with his head on his folded arms. He awoke when Oliver uttered loudly, 'Excuse me,' and hastily pulled himself together, rubbing his eyes with the tips of his fingers.

'Is the restaurant open?'

'No open.'

Oliver called out to Ronald, who was examining the tyres of his car, parked outside the entrance. 'No food available. What about spending the night here?'

'Have they rooms?'

'The place seems empty.' Oliver turned to the young man, 'Have you two rooms for tonight?'

'The manager he sleep. I cannot say. He wake up four o'clock, five o'clock. He tell you.'

'Can't you ask him now?'

'No.' The lad's negative was firm and he could not be persuaded to awaken the manager.

'He must be afraid of him,' said Ronald to Oliver as they were walking towards the ruins.

While they were stumbling among the unspectacular remains of the temples, Ronald, who had a guide book, informed his companion that Cyrene was founded in the 7th century BC and at the height of its prosperity its inhabitants numbered over 100,000.

'And I'd never heard of the place,' Oliver admitted. 'How ignorant one is,' he added, modestly. 'The ruins aren't up to much though.'

'No,' replied Ronald. 'But the site is full of ancient history. In its heyday it was as important as Delphi.'

On their return to the hotel, they discovered that the manager had risen from his siesta and didn't do much more than sit at the reception desk and order about the boy, who had been minding the place during his afternoon rest. The manager, an

Egyptian, had a relaxed attitude to his job. The travellers were allotted two adjacent rooms, shown to them by the boy, also Egyptian, whose knowing smile suggested that he had their measure. The boy served them (they were the only guests) a meal consisting of tinned consommé, well diluted by hot water, tinned spaghetti in tomato sauce and tinned pears. During the meal Ronald chatted to the boy in Arabic, to Oliver's irritation.

'What are you saying to him?' asked Oliver, envious.

'Just passing the time of day,' replied Ronald. 'His name is Ahmed, he comes from Alexandria and has five brothers and three sisters. He's seventeen and he's been here four months.'

'It's extraordinary how good looking and stalwart the poor Egyptians are,' remarked Oliver.

'They soon put on weight if they get a sedentary job. Look at the manager.'

'Khalid didn't. He kept his figure,' said Oliver.

There was nothing to do except to go to bed after the meal as the lights in the place were too weak to read by.

Oliver retired first. Ronald noticed that Oliver's door was ajar when he passed his room on the way to his own and he left his door ajar too.

When they had ground up the steep escarpment and joined the road to Benghazi, Ronald said, 'I noticed you left your door open last night. Did Ahmed join you?'

'Alas, no. Did he visit you?' asked Oliver.

'No, in spite of my hints.'

'And in Arabic?'

'Yes, and in Arabic.'

'Too bad,' said Oliver, pleased that Ronald's knowledge had not won him any favours.

They drove on in silence past the remains of Italian farms. Ronald said, 'This used to be the granary of the Roman Empire.'

'Why is it so derelict?'

'The Italians have gone. The Arabs are Bedouin. They like to wander and camp here and there.'

After covering another stretch, Oliver took over the driving from Ronald. 'I wonder what's happened to Violet and Joan.'

'I expect they're making passionate love in a five-star hotel in Tripoli,' said Ronald.

'How will we find them?'

'The Jaguar will stick out like a double-decker bus.'

'I don't like my Jaguar being compared to a bus,' objected Oliver.

'What I meant was that it will probably be the only Jaguar in Tripoli,' replied Ronald, sleepily.

☪

'*Darling!*' exclaimed Violet.

'Yes?' answered Joan, sharply; she hated being called 'darling' by Violet; if the endearment had been uttered by Saman it would have been different; Saman, though, did not have many terms of endearment in his vocabulary.

They were having breakfast in their bedroom at the Libya Palace Hotel in Tripoli. Joan had weakened and consented to share a room, partly because doing so meant that Violet would pay for it and not ask her to stump up as she did when they had two rooms. She was rather short of money and the Libyans were not interested in having Egyptian pounds.

'Darling,' repeated Violet.

'Yes?' repeated Joan a little less sharply.

'We must go to Leptis Magna.'

'Today, d'you mean? I should go home.'

'It seems quite quiet here. We can see about our forward journey tomorrow. Oliver and Ronald should be here by then.'

'How will we meet them?'

'We'll run into them, I'm sure.'

☪

The hotel that Oliver and Ronald stayed in at Benghazi was an improvement on the one in Cyrene, less informal and more what a hotel should be. The next morning they began the several-hundred-mile drive to Tripoli. The desert journey was monotonous and uneventful. The villages they passed through seemed tumbledown and miserable. At Sirte there was a sort of hotel but it was still under reconstruction and half-closed. No accomodation was available and the restaurant was only able to provide spaghetti doused in a chilli sauce.

'Quite disgusting,' pronounced Oliver. 'My mouth is on fire.'

They reached Leptis Magna at midnight and parked in a little square outside the entrance to the ruins. Ronald slept on a bench; Oliver in the car.

While Oliver was photographing the back view of the statue of an ephebe that stands out among the ruins of the ancient city, there came a loud cry of 'Hello there!' and soon Violet and Joan joined Oliver and Ronald.

Oliver quickly slipped his camera into its case.

'Where on earth did you spend the night?' asked Violet.

'Here.'

'Is there a hotel?'

'We slept rough,' said Ronald.

'What news?' asked Oliver of his wife.

'News?' queried Violet, puzzled.

'About the situation.'

'Oh that. I don't know. Tripoli seems to be all right.'

'There were two Englishmen,' put in Joan, 'in the hotel. They seemed worried.'

'Oh stop fussing about those dreary businessmen, Joan.'

'They live in Tripoli. They should know.'

Oliver and Ronald, having thoroughly inspected Leptis Magna before Violet's and Joan's arrival, drove on to the Libya Palace Hotel, leaving the two women to do their sightseeing by themselves. The men were anxious to have a bath and a decent meal.

At the hotel they were told by Mr Henning, the polite German manager, that there was only one room, a twin-bedded one, available; they took it without enthusiasm.

'It's absurd,' said Ronald, after the porter had deposited their baggage in their room, 'that we should share a room while your wife is shacking up with Joan. You should be in Violet's room.'

'God forbid!' replied Oliver. 'And should Joan move in with you?'

'Heavens no!'

'Then what? The manager said that this was the only room they had.'

'Managers always have a room up their sleeve,' rejoined Ronald, unhelpfully.

The conversation among the four at dinner was like that of fellow passengers who have only just met on a ship. They discussed their journeys, until Oliver said to Violet, 'I can't understand why you didn't wait for us somewhere, instead of pushing on as if we didn't exist.'

'Impatience propelled me,' she replied with a smile.

'We might have broken down, had an accident.'

'I knew you'd get through all right,' went on Violet, 'in Ronald's reliable little car.'

'How could you know?'

'If we hadn't met you at Leptis Magna, we would have gone back to look for you, wouldn't we, Joan?'

'For God's sake let's stop talking about what happened. I want to know what we are going to do. I want to go home.' Joan seemed overwrought.

Violet addressed her husband. 'She's tired after the journey. She was a good girl. She didn't fall asleep while I was driving.'

'I'm tired too,' complained Oliver.

Ronald said, 'I suppose it's all right parking in the street. I put my car outside the hotel, opposite the entrance.'

'Mine's in a side street,' said Violet, smugly.

'I've an idea,' announced Ronald. 'I suggest we motor to Tunisia and catch a boat from Tunis to Marseilles.'

'I've had enough of car travel,' said Joan, pointedly, looking at her plate of half-eaten *poulet fricassé*.

'It seems perfectly quiet here,' said Violet. 'I suggest we stay for a few days. An American group checked in yesterday—'

'I heard them,' interrupted Oliver. 'Why do Americans have to talk so loud?'

'It's to reassure themselves of their existence,' explained Ronald.

'As I was saying,' contined Violet, 'an American group arrived yesterday. Americans are timid tourists. It's unlikely that they would come here if there were going to be trouble.'

'How could they know?' asked Oliver.

'Their embassy would tell them,' replied Violet authoritatively.

☪

The next morning the quartet, more in discord than in harmony, left the hotel on foot making their way towards the main street. Joan wanted a ticket to London; Ronald wanted information about the road to Tunisia; Violet wanted to find out about visiting Sabratha, and Oliver didn't know what he wanted except to buy a stamp for a postcard he had written to his mother. They soon came upon the post office and they all went into the building, where Oliver bought a stamp.

On leaving the post office, the four stopped at the top of the steps. There came a huge roar and a wild, raging crowd of Libyans brandishing clubs and sticks stormed past yelling and screaming and torching cars. An Arab, also a customer at the post office told Ronald, who had spoken to him in Arabic, in English that war had broken out between the Arabs and Israel, and the demonstrators were probably making their way to the American and British embassies to protest about the pro-Israeli policy of the USA and Britain.

The clamorous crowd continued to howl past. It was like a savage monster, its members intoxicated by the fervour of their fury.

'We'd better wait until they've gone by and then make for the hotel,' advised Ronald.

Many cars were burning. 'I hope the Jaguar is all right,' said Oliver.

When the mob had stormed away the four hastened towards the Libya Palace Hotel via the side street where the Jaguar had been parked; the vehicle was ablaze.

'Oh dear, what are we going to do?' said Violet, whose self-control and sang-froid prevented her from showing any emotion; to her the loss of the expensive car was an inconvenience rather then a financial blow. 'It will be a write off.'

'Insurance,' soothed Oliver, more to himself than anyone else.

They hurried past the burning wreck and gained the safety of the hotel, guarded by a posse of police. In the lobby the American tourists were assembled. Most of them were on the verge of panic. Their guide, an Englishman, tried to calm them. 'Remember, ladies and gentlemen,' he cried, 'that this is called "an adventure tour".'

'We didn't bargain for this,' objected a well-covered matron in a wide-brimmed straw hat. 'You must get in touch with the Consul and tell him to rescue us. It's dangerous to stay here with all those burning cars around.'

'The Consul is on his way. He'll arrange to take you all to the American army base.'

Violet and Oliver went to the reception desk and asked a surly Libyan clerk to summon the manager. Mr Henning soon appeared. He seemed harassed but he did not allow his obvious concern to deprive him of his professional courtesy. 'I am very sorry, madame. When the situation has calmed down you can lodge a complaint about your car with the appropriate authority.'

'That won't do much good, will it?' remarked Oliver.

'Probably not, but you can try.'

'What should we do?' asked Oliver. 'My car has gone, our only form of transport.'

'I suggest you stay here,' advised the manager. 'The hotel has a police guard and we should be safe.'

A bus arrived to take the Americans to their army base. The Consul, lanky, bespectacled, grey-faced, and the guide conducted the tourists to the bus. The porters paid little respect to the tourists' luggage, hurling the suitcases into the back of the bus as if their contents were *haram*.

The quartet went up to the roof of the hotel. The two English businessmen, whom Violet and Joan had met before, were watching the fires that were burning all over the town.

'That's the Jewish-owned cinema,' said one pointing.

'And that's a Jewish petrol station,' said the other also pointing.

'They're going for Jewish property,' remarked Ronald.

'My car's been set on fire,' Violet told the businessmen; one was dark and short with glasses; the other tall, fair and balding; both were in their late forties.

'Bad luck,' said the short businessman.

'It was a Jaguar,' Oliver told them.

'They go for the posh cars,' said the tall businessman.

'Mine escaped,' said Ronald. 'It was outside the hotel.'

'What was it?' asked the short businessman.

'A small Fiat.'

'Oh well,' said the tall businessman as if it wouldn't have mattered if it had been incinerated.

'How long will this last?' asked Joan anxiously.

'A few days, a few years. Who knows?'

'I have to get back to England,' said Joan.

'The airport is closed,' said the tall businessman.

The Six Day War had begun. At first a victory for the Arabs was reported; soon, however, that news proved to be false. Arab over-confidence was destroyed. The staff at the hotel – except for the Italian room maid – became hostile and the service perfunctory, bordering on the rude.

'We must get out of here,' said Violet, wriggling her shoulders as if to rid herself of something nasty on her back. The four were at the bar trying to order a drink from the sullen barman, who seemed not to notice them.

'But how?' asked Ronald.

'You said something about motoring to Tunisia . . .'

'Yes, but now your car's a write off. How can we?'

'In your car. It has four seats.'

'But what about the luggage?'

'On the roof,' said Violet at once.

'I haven't got a rack.'

'Then get one.'

'How? The place is shut down.'

'You can try. Ask the manager.'

During this exchange between Violet and Ronald, Oliver and Joan remained silent. At the end Joan perked up with, 'I want to fly to London.'

'Didn't one of those businessmen say the airport was closed?' said Oliver.

'It may reopen,' Joan replied optimistically.

☪

'It's simply not possible for me to take all four of us and the luggage in my car,' Ronald said to Oliver in their bedroom. They were both undressing after an unsatisfactory dinner, which they had eaten in silence following an argument about driving to Tunisia in the Fiat.

'I can see your point,' admitted Oliver.

'I didn't realize she could be so bossy.'

'She gets her own way,' said Oliver ruefully,

'I don't know how you can stand it.'

'We get on all right when we don't see too much of each other. I agree with you, Ronald. The stay in Cairo was too long. She gets impatient, takes it out on me. Joan is one of the causes of her discontent. Joan's probably rebuffed her.'

When the two had completed their ablutions and got into their separate beds, Ronald put down *Middlemarch*, which he had just opened, and said, 'Shall we run away? Go off without Violet and Joan. Drive to Tunisia in my car.'

'I can't do that, as much as I would like to.'

'Violet drove off without waiting for us.'

'We did have your car,' said Oliver, 'and we were going in the same direction. We can't abandon Violet and Joan without transport.'

'They could fly back to London. The airport is bound to reopen soon.' Ronald took up his book.

'How you can read that boring stuff I can't think.'

'It's one of my favourites, Dorothea and Causubon are wonderfully drawn characters, aren't they?'

'I've never read the book,' confessed Oliver. 'Anyway as you've read it before, it can hold no surprises for you, so you might turn out your bedside lamp. Goodnight.'

☪

'I want to fly back to London,' said Joan to the others at breakfast in the Libya Palace Hotel.

'You can't,' replied Violet. 'The airport is closed.'

'The manager told me this morning that it had reopened,' said Joan meekly.

'Did he really?' Oliver said with surprise and interest.

'But all planes are fully booked,' went on Joan.

'I can't fly. I have my car,' put in Ronald.

'We'll keep to our plan,' said Violet, emphatically.

'I didn't know we had a plan,' mumbled Oliver.

'To motor in Ronald's car to Tunisia.' Violet regarded Ronald. 'Did you get the luggage rack?'

'No. Like you I was all day in the hotel.'

'We'll start tomorrow,' Violet told her companions. 'You can see about the rack this morning, after you have taken me to the British Consulate. I must report the incineration of my car.'

'I don't know how I can get a rack if all the shops are closed,' said Ronald. 'Why don't you and Joan wait for a flight to London. Oliver and I can motor to Tunisia. My little car isn't big enough for four. There's no leg room at the back.'

'I'll sit in front,' answered Violet, firmly. 'And I can help with the driving.'

'I think I'll fly back with Joan.' Oliver turned to Joan and added, 'You'd like that, wouldn't you?'

Joan gave Oliver a puzzled look and said nothing.

'How's the war going?' asked Violet.

'I heard the BBC news on my Sony transistor set,' Ronald informed the party. 'It seems that the Israelis are winning.'

'Oh dear! There'll be trouble if the Arabs are defeated. We must go as soon as possible. 'Violet got up from the breakfast table and made for the reception desk. Ronald followed her.

Joan started to rise.

'Oh don't go, Joan,' said Oliver. 'Stay until I've finished my coffee. Why don't you have that last piece of toast? I don't want it.'

'I want to fly back to London,' Joan said, not for the first time.

'We all know that, dear.'

'I don't want to motor to Tunisia with Violet in Ronald's car.'

'We know that too.'

'What shall I do?' Joan was tearful. 'She's really terrible.'

'Violet, d'you mean?'

'She likes to control everyone.'

Oliver sighed. 'Don't I know it.'

'Why do you let her run you?'

'Money,' replied Oliver.

☪

At the reception desk Violet was speaking with — or, more correctly — browbeating Mr Henning, the manager, who did not show any sign of irritation or fluster. 'We must get a luggage rack,' Violet was saying, 'Can you help?'

'I'll see.'

'Are there any taxis?'

'I'm not sure.'

Violet turned to Ronald, who was by her side. 'You'll have to take me to the Consulate.' To the manager she added, 'See about the luggage rack, please,' and to Ronald, 'Let's go.'

Ronald obeyed the order and drove Violet to the British Consulate.

Meanwhile, Oliver sat smoking a rare after-breakfast cigarette in the lounge; he never dared smoke in Violet's presence. From where he sat he could see through the glass doors into the lobby. Joan, who had gone upstairs a while ago, appeared with one of the porters and her bags. They hurried towards the front door.

Oliver heaved himself out of his armchair with unaccustomed alacrity and hastened after her. She was getting into a car when he reached the bottom step of the hotel entrance.

'Where are you going, Joan?'

'Malta,' she replied with a sly smile.

'But all the planes are full, aren't they?'

'The hotel travel bureau got me a cancellation on a plane to Malta. The man said I was very lucky.'

'The hotel travel bureau? I didn't know there was one. What about Violet?'

'She's old enough to look after herself, and she has you. I must go. The plane leaves in under an hour and I have to pick up my ticket at the airport.'

'You're being very independent.'

'For a change.' She got into the taxi and closed the door. 'Goodbye,' she cried out of the window. 'Give my regards to your *wife*.'

The car drove off.

Oliver stood for a minute as if in a daze, and then he laughed. 'She's cleverer than I thought,' he muttered to himself. He remounted the steps and at the reception desk asked for the manager. 'I see that Miss Webber has left.' he said to the obliging German. 'She told me she had got a flight to Malta.'

'That's right.'

'She seems to have left without telling any of her companions. Did she pay her bill?'

'She said that Mrs Brent would look after it.'

'Or I will. I couldn't share my wife's room as Miss Webber could hardly share with Mr Wood. There was only one room available when Mr Wood and I arrived.'

'We have plenty of vacant rooms now the American group has gone.'

'May I have a room to myself? My wife snores and keeps me awake.' Oliver gave a nervous laugh. 'We usually sleep in separate rooms because of her trumpeting.' Oliver laughed again, but Mr Henning remained serious. 'I'll see what can be done,' he promised.

Violet and Ronald did not return from the Consulate until well after noon and Violet came back in a fury.

'We had to *wait*,' complained Violet to Oliver, who had been dozing in the lounge and spotted them when they entered the lobby. She turned to Ronald. 'You'd better see about the rack. Where's Joan?'

'She's gone,' said Oliver, unable to hide his glee.

'Gone? Gone where?'

'Flown to Malta.'

'Malta! But the planes are all full, aren't they?'

'She managed to get a cancellation,' explained Oliver.

'I'll fly to Malta. Arrange it, Oliver.' Violet ascended to her room.

'I suppose we'd better obey commands,' said Oliver to Ronald, starting towards the hotel travel bureau.

'Since Joan's flown and Violet's flying, I shan't do anything about that bloody luggage rack Violet keeps on about. Will you fly with her, or drive with me?'

Oliver paused as if to struggle to make a decision, and then blurted out, 'I'll come with you, of course.'

'Good. I'm looking forward to Tunisia.'

☪

In Cairo Cedric was busy reporting the war with Israel, which ended in disaster for the Arabs, who lost Sinai, the West Bank of the River Jordan and the Golan Heights, the Syrian range that looked down upon Israel and which the Israelis had coveted for a long time; the Israelis were also on the East Bank of the Suez Canal. The Egyptian government tried to put a brave face on the dire situation euphemistically calling it a 'setback'; it was in fact a catastrophic defeat.

Cairo itself did not suffer much; a few bombs were dropped here and there in the suburbs causing little damage. The damage that was done, apart from the enormous losses borne by the Egyptian army and air force, was to the self-esteem of

Oliver heaved himself out of his armchair with unaccustomed alacrity and hastened after her. She was getting into a car when he reached the bottom step of the hotel entrance.

'Where are you going, Joan?'

'Malta,' she replied with a sly smile.

'But all the planes are full, aren't they?'

'The hotel travel bureau got me a cancellation on a plane to Malta. The man said I was very lucky.'

'The hotel travel bureau? I didn't know there was one. What about Violet?'

'She's old enough to look after herself, and she has you. I must go. The plane leaves in under an hour and I have to pick up my ticket at the airport.'

'You're being very independent.'

'For a change.' She got into the taxi and closed the door. 'Goodbye,' she cried out of the window. 'Give my regards to your *wife*.'

The car drove off.

Oliver stood for a minute as if in a daze, and then he laughed. 'She's cleverer than I thought,' he muttered to himself. He remounted the steps and at the reception desk asked for the manager. 'I see that Miss Webber has left.' he said to the obliging German. 'She told me she had got a flight to Malta.'

'That's right.'

'She seems to have left without telling any of her companions. Did she pay her bill?'

'She said that Mrs Brent would look after it.'

'Or I will. I couldn't share my wife's room as Miss Webber could hardly share with Mr Wood. There was only one room available when Mr Wood and I arrived.'

'We have plenty of vacant rooms now the American group has gone.'

'May I have a room to myself? My wife snores and keeps me awake.' Oliver gave a nervous laugh. 'We usually sleep in separate rooms because of her trumpeting.' Oliver laughed again, but Mr Henning remained serious. 'I'll see what can be done,' he promised.

Violet and Ronald did not return from the Consulate until well after noon and Violet came back in a fury.

'We had to *wait*,' complained Violet to Oliver, who had been dozing in the lounge and spotted them when they entered the lobby. She turned to Ronald. 'You'd better see about the rack. Where's Joan?'

'She's gone,' said Oliver, unable to hide his glee.

'Gone? Gone where?'

'Flown to Malta.'

'Malta! But the planes are all full, aren't they?'

'She managed to get a cancellation,' explained Oliver.

'I'll fly to Malta. Arrange it, Oliver.' Violet ascended to her room.

'I suppose we'd better obey commands,' said Oliver to Ronald, starting towards the hotel travel bureau.

'Since Joan's flown and Violet's flying, I shan't do anything about that bloody luggage rack Violet keeps on about. Will you fly with her, or drive with me?'

Oliver paused as if to struggle to make a decision, and then blurted out, 'I'll come with you, of course.'

'Good. I'm looking forward to Tunisia.'

☪

In Cairo Cedric was busy reporting the war with Israel, which ended in disaster for the Arabs, who lost Sinai, the West Bank of the River Jordan and the Golan Heights, the Syrian range that looked down upon Israel and which the Israelis had coveted for a long time; the Israelis were also on the East Bank of the Suez Canal. The Egyptian government tried to put a brave face on the dire situation euphemistically calling it a 'setback'; it was in fact a catastrophic defeat.

Cairo itself did not suffer much; a few bombs were dropped here and there in the suburbs causing little damage. The damage that was done, apart from the enormous losses borne by the Egyptian army and air force, was to the self-esteem of the Arabs. However, a resilient people, they resigned themselves to their humiliation.

Nasser spoke to the nation admitting the shattering defeat and announcing his resignation. This announcement brought thousands of Cairenes into the streets. They demanded that he stay and stay he did. Cedric joined the crowds crying, 'Gamal, Gamal' and shared the exhilaration of the jellaba-clad citizens, who were defying the defeat. Cedric had no fear of milling with the crowd, none of whom showed any antagonism to his presence among them.

The situation in Cairo became grim; there were shortages and rationing; the Cairenes used to deprivation and hardship bore the restrictions stoically. Cedric was pleased to live among the long-suffering residents of the great capital. Groppi's did not close its doors, but had to curtail its menu.

☪

Violet descended to the lobby accompanied by the three hotel porters and her luggage. She spotted Oliver sitting in the travel agent's office and went up to him.

'There's little chance of a plane to Malta today or tomorrow, A general strike has been declared,' Oliver told his wife.

Unperturbed, Violet said, 'Then we'll have to go back to our original plan and motor to Tunisia in Ronald's car. Did he get the rack fixed?'

'I don't think so.'

'But he said he was going to,' objected Violet.

'He thought it wouldn't be necessary as you were flying to Malta.'

'I'm not now,' she said crossly. 'So it is necessary. Anyway I expect Joan will get a flight from Malta to London. Where is Ronald?'

'Upstairs, I think, reading *Middlemarch*.'

'Huh! He seems oblivious to the crisis. Go and tell him to see about the rack. We must leave at dawn tomorrow if not this afternoon.' Violet left the office and returned to her room with the porters and her luggage.

Later, the party, now reduced to three, met at dinner in the hotel. All the kitchen could produce was a dish of boiled rice and cold chicken followed by tinned peaches. Violet went on about the luggage rack and Ronald prevaricated.

'If you don't get it we can't go tomorrow.'

'The travel agent,' said Ronald, 'has just told me there's an Italian ship in port sailing tomorrow afternoon to Naples and calling at Malta and Syracuse on the way. Why don't we take that? There's a drive-on arrangement for cars.'

Violet thought for a moment, playing with a slice of tinned peach. She looked at Ronald and smiled, 'Of course we must. Joan may not have got a plane to London. We'll stay at the Phoenicia in Valetta. It's quite good. Oliver and I stayed there once. D'you remember, Oliver?'

'Yes. Malta is one of the few largish islands about which one feels one should say "on" instead of "in". It's so flat.'

'How can the boat sail if there's a strike?' asked Violet, after thought.

'Apparently the dock people don't strike,' replied Ronald.

'That's unusual,' put in Oliver.

It was agreed that they should try to get berths on the boat to Malta the next morning.

☪

Oliver had moved out of Ronald's room and moved into one of his own. Violet approved of his not wanting to share with her.

Ronald couldn't sleep. He thought of Oliver and Violet and decided he had had enough of them, but how could he escape from their clutches? He began to feel ashamed of his having run away from Cairo. Cedric had stayed on in spite of the Consul's warning to British residents. And there was Khalid, who couldn't leave. Suddenly, Ronald made up his mind. He leapt out of bed and started to pack. When he had finished, he rang the front desk, told the clerk on night duty he was leaving at once and asked him to prepare his bill. A sleepy porter came up and took Ronald's bags down and loaded them into the Fiat after Ronald had paid the bill and tipped the clerk generously. He wrote a note to Oliver: 'Sorry to let you down. I feel a coward so am going back to Egypt. Bon voyage! I hope you get that boat.'

He gave several banknotes to the night porter and set off on the long journey to Cairo. It was three o'clock in the morning. The city was quiet and the guards at the check points let him through without any trouble.

☪

Violet was furious about Ronald's flight; Oliver was sympathetic but he didn't express his feelings to his wife; instead, he weakly agreed with her excoriation of Ronald.

'How dare he!' Violet said to her husband when they met the next morning in the lobby. 'It's sheer selfishness to leave us in the lurch. I had thought he was a reasonable person and a friend. It was cowardly and ungentlemanly of him to sneak away like a thief in the middle of the night. Wasn't he at school with you? Unforgiveable. I hope never to see him again.'

'At least he found out about the Italian boat,' rejoined Oliver in an attempt to mollify his irate wife.

☪

'So you're back!' said Cedric to Ronald as he took a seat opposite his friend, who was already installed on a banquette in Groppi's.

'Yes, as you see, I'm back.'

'But why? D'you mean to say you went all the way to Tripoli and back?'

'Yes. I felt I'd been a coward to leave the sinking ship.'

'Well, it hasn't sunk yet, not completely anyway. Egypt is in a pretty bad way. The people, though, are still behind Nasser. They need their father figure. What will you do? The schools are closed for the holidays.'

'Can you get me a job, Cedric?'

'I'll see. The paper needs, or at least I need, an English assistant.'

'I don't want to go back to Nile College, even if they'd have me. I would, though, like to stay here and suffer with the Egyptians. A little austerity would do me good. I'm sure I could get that ghastly flat back. I've put up temporarily at the Green Valley Hotel in Sarwat Pasha street.'

'The Green Valley? I used to stay there. Is Roberto still the manager?'

'Yes.'

'He's a good fellow. Many people have begun their Cairo careers in the Green Valley—'

'And ended there?'

'No, they usually move on before they end.'

☪

The Italian ship sailed from Tripoli as scheduled, and the Brents were aboard. The Phoenicia Hotel in Valetta, though, was full. Violet and Oliver, after a long session in a tourist office with an unhelpful young, pregnant clerk, who seemed to resent having to help find accomodation since it meant her having to struggle to her feet to get pamphlets, found two rooms in a guest-house whose one redeeming feature was its view over the Grand Harbour. Violet visited other hotels and travel agencies in a futile search for Joan. After a few days the couple flew to England.

☪

Joan had already contacted Saman, now in Bangkok. They had spoken on the phone every day and Saman had succeeded in persuading her to join him in Thailand. He was so charming, persuasive and irresistible on the phone that it was impossible to refuse him; hearing his dulcet voice made her skin tingle with excitement. She longed for him. Her father complained about her calls to Bangkok though she reversed the charges, and also his calls from Bangkok which sometimes came in the middle of the night. He did not want his daughter to go far away now she had just come home, but he was unable to prevent her.

☪

'I came back because of you,' Ronald told Khalid when they were in bed together in the Green Valley Hotel.

'I love you, Mister Ron. When I get your money and your letter from the *bawab* I cry.'

'Dear Khalid,' murmured Ronald, holding the young man's firm, glabrous body.

After the bath when they were drinking local brandy, Khalid said, 'May I ask you a question, Mister Ron?'

'Of course, my dear.'

'Can you help me go to Australia?'

'Australia?' His tone reminded him of Algernon's exclamation in the second act of *The Importance of Being Earnest*. He laughed, but it was pointless to tell the puzzled Khalid why.

'Mister Ron, nothing in Egypt. Australia have good jobs. I have friend who go to Sydney and he happy there.'

'But what could you do there, Khalid? It would be difficult to get a job in a bank. Your English isn't good enough.'

'I not work in bank in Australia, I work in building. I become welder. My friend he say that construction business need worker like me.'

'But you know nothing about welding. It requires learning. You need to learn the skill. It's a dangerous job anyway.'

'I can learn easy. Will you help me?'

'I'm not Australian and I don't know anyone in Australia. How can I help you?'

'You can write letter, say you know me, say I good welder. You do that for me, Mister Ron?'

'Yes, I suppose so.'

'Mister Ron, I love you.'